VORACIOUS

VORACIOUS

WRATH JAMES WHITE

CEMETERY DANCE PUBLICATIONS

Baltimore
2024

Cemetery Dance Publications
132B Industry Lane, Unit #7
Forest Hill, MD 21050
www.cemeterydance.com

Trade Paperback Edition

ISBN:
978-1-58767-953-7

Cover Artwork and Design © 2024 by Justin Coons
Cover and Interior Design © 2024 by Desert Isle Design, LLC

**L**ELANI SIMMS woke up hungry, terribly, overwhelmingly hungry. It felt as if her entire world would end if she didn't eat something, anything, everything she could, now. The hunger consumed her thoughts, allowing no other considerations or concerns. Career, family, society, the latest political squabble or celebrity divorce—none of it mattered. Nothing mattered except the pain churning in the pit of her gut.

Shadows danced across the walls, dark chimeras caused by the traffic below and the lights of the other high-rise condos and office buildings. A crack of lightning sent the shadows off in a riot through the apartment. It was the kind of night that used to frighten Lelani out of her wits and cause her to sleep with all the lights on. But on this night, she was oblivious to all but the cloying pain in her belly. The flashes of lightning seemed to coincide with the hunger pains, as if there was a link between the two, the lancing jolts of pain in her gut so intense that it left her flesh and arced across the sky.

It was past one a.m. and Lelani had not slept more than an hour at a time in the last forty-eight. Her hunger had prevented all but the briefest naps. Lelani's refrigerator stood open, the light calling out to her, cutting a swath through the shadows and guiding her to salvation. But it was a barren wasteland of empty cartons and containers leaking their remaining contents down into the vegetable bins in a congealing stew of rotting perishables. She had opened every box and can and completely gutted the freezer. A mere thirty minutes had passed since the last time she had eaten, yet Lelani was ravenous. She had scrambled a dozen eggs, fried three hamburger patties, and boiled an entire pack of hotdogs and gobbled down still another pack uncooked. Then she drank a gallon of milk and made six peanut butter and jelly sandwiches before falling asleep on the couch. When Lelani woke thirty minutes later, she felt as if she hadn't eaten in months.

Her metabolism had always been fast. Even now that she was in her mid-thirties and maintaining her runway figure had become a daily battle, she was aware that, by the standards of the average woman, Lelani was practically anorexic. By the harsh standards of the fashion industry, however, she was practically a cow. She had blown up to 120 pounds, ten pounds heavier than her ideal weight, and getting the weight off and keeping it off had been her crucible the last few years. That wasn't a problem anymore.

Lelani hadn't felt this hungry during her most extreme diets. Liquid diets, raw food diets, vegan and macrobiotic diets, even when she'd restricted her calorie intake to barely enough to sustain a hummingbird, fewer than five hundred calories a day, she hadn't felt this ravenous. Her latest medical weight remedy had left her with a metabolism like a star going nova. Food was all she could think of. It was her only priority. And no matter how much she ate, the weight continued to melt away.

Today she had lost another six pounds and was half-mad with a gnawing, insatiable hunger combined with sleep deprivation. She felt like a prisoner of war. Ever since the hunger had advanced beyond the persistent, nagging ache, which had been seventy-two hours ago to the desperate agonizing imperative it was now, she had been unable to order her thoughts. She had hallucinations and blackouts and long periods when her thoughts drifted in no coherent order, when she was just barely conscious. She was exhausted. It was torture. A living hell. Her flesh burned as her body cannibalized itself, eating away the last vestiges of fat and beginning to feed on her muscle tissue. Only eating seemed to calm the fire within her, but that only lasted a short while before the burning hunger returned like an incurable, recurring infection. Kicking heroin had not felt this bad.

Her stomach had shrunk and was now concave, sucked in against her pelvis and ribcage, rumbling audibly. In the silence of the night, it sounded like the purr of a large jungle cat. Lelani's arms and legs were completely devoid of adipose tissue, and most of the muscle tissue had atrophied, the skin drawn tight to knobby bones. They resembled something insectoid, like the jointed limbs of a spider. Her cheekbones jutted like axe blades from her skeletal face. Her fingers were bony claws, with nails grown long and gnarled. Her hair was a frizzled nest of tangled knaps.

It had only been eight years since Lelani was voted one of the most beautiful women in the world. But there were fathoms between twenty-eight and thirty-six. At twenty-eight, she could eat whatever she wanted and starve herself back to a size one in a few days. At thirty-six, it took a full-time personal trainer, a nutritionist, and a plastic surgeon to keep her off the unemployment line. Born in Hawaii to a mother of mixed Japanese and Hawaiian descent and a father who was African American and Irish, Lelani had inherited the most desirable physical attributes of both. Her skin was a blemish-free, light cappuccino tan. Her eyes were hazel and slightly slanted. Her lips were full and bow-shaped. Her hair was long, curly, and raven black. She was tall and naturally slender, with muscular legs and arms and an ass that sat up high and tight like that of an Olympic sprinter. Her exotic looks and signature gaunt "heroin chic" appearance had made her one of the fashion industry's most sought-after models.

Then she'd begun gaining weight, and the tabloids had not been kind. As her weight yo-yoed, capturing a photo of her looking flabby, a shot of her in a bikini with a paunch or conspicuous cellulite had become the holy grail of the paparazzi. She had grown increasingly desperate and had finally sought medical help. Now, she had wasted away to nothing. Beyond even "runway skinny," she looked like she was a pound or two from organ failure, like something that had clawed itself out of the grave. Her famous, muscular gluteus maximus was now a mere coccyx draped in a parchment-thin layer of skin. Her breasts were two withered bladders, shriveled up on her chest like dried peaches. She looked like death's diseased mistress.

Lelani's eyes shined like mirrors, catching the faint glow from the streetlights and reflecting it into the night like some nocturnal beast. She scampered off the couch on all fours. Saliva tinged with red dripped from elongated canines tipped with red, giving her the appearance of a vampire—if vampirism was accompanied by anorexia and a complete disregard for personal hygiene. Lelani smelled like an animal. She hadn't bathed since the hunger had begun. She hadn't done anything but eat and sleep.

Lelani raced into the kitchen and attacked the remaining food. She opened the last cans of corn and dumped them into her mouth while she searched for something else to consume. She opened a half-frozen bag of peas and carrots and began shoveling its contents into her mouth in large handfuls, whimpering at the soothing feeling of the much-needed nourishment, but she needed more.

She needed meat.

She looked around the kitchen. In the sink was an open package of frozen chicken breasts. She had taken it out of the freezer earlier and tried to eat it, but it had been too frozen, so Lelani had placed it in a sink filled with warm water to thaw it. She pulled the package out of the sink and pulled off a piece of chicken breast. It was still partially frozen. She ran it under water so hot it nearly scalded her. Then she shoved the cold, dead poultry into her mouth and began to chew, heedless of the fact that she hadn't cooked it yet. The raw meat tasted good. It was nourishment. Calories. That's all that concerned her now. Lelani repeated the process until the entire package was gone and her stomach was filled, and then she returned to the couch and collapsed once more into a deep, dreamless slumber.

Like an alarm clock, Lelani woke exactly thirty minutes later. The room spun and blurred. Lelani barely knew where she was. She struggled to her feet and shuffled forward, exhausted. Her stomach growled. She moved quickly toward the kitchen in an awkward shuffle. Lelani looked at the countertops piled high with empty cans, containers, and boxes and then opened the freezer and stared at the bare shelves. There was no food. Even the condiments—the mayonnaise, ketchup, mustard, horseradish, Tabasco sauce, and soy sauce containers were empty. There was no food anywhere. She practically ran to the cupboard. It too was empty except for a few eight-ounce cans of designer cat food. Lelani seized those, opened them, and quickly shoveled their contents into her mouth, barely tasting the flavorless gruel as she licked each can clean.

When she'd eaten the last can, she looked around and spotted more cat food in a dish by the cat door leading out to the yard. She dropped down on all fours and scarfed it down.

It wasn't enough. Her stomach still growled. The pain still churned in her guts like a belly full of barbed wire. She stood up and ran for her car keys. She needed to get more food. The nearest supermarket was six miles away and the nearest late-night restaurant was at least seven. She calculated the time it would take to drive there in traffic, find parking, and purchase food. Twenty minutes to get to the supermarket, find something to eat, and make it through the checkout line if she pushed it, and it would take more than an hour to get seated and served if she went to a restaurant. Too long. She needed to eat now.

Lelani began to moan, a low, mournful dirge. She dropped to her knees and wept uncontrollably. Her mind fragmented into a thousand jagged shards, every one feeling like they were working their way through her digestive system.

"Oh, God! I'm so fucking hungry! What the hell is wrong with me? What did they do to me? Why is this happening?"

This was her first coherent thought in hours. A sliver of sanity that she grasped like a lifesaver in a swirling maelstrom of pain and ravenous appetite. Then her mind lost all cohesion once more. Lelani clawed at her arms and face before pounding her fists on the floor in frustration. She grabbed the keys again and stood up, determined to make it to the supermarket and feed herself and restock her pantry and refrigerator if she had to break a speed record to do it.

She reached for the front door when she heard the pet door that led out to the balcony open. Prince Charles, her pedigree Himalayan, entered the kitchen with a quizzical, "Meow?"

Lelani dropped down on all fours and scuttled into the kitchen on her long bony limbs. She spotted Prince Charles sitting in the center of the kitchen floor, licking his empty food bowl. Lelani pounced. She tackled the kitten like she was trying to take down an NFL quarterback. They slid across the marble tiles, through the empty food wrappers and containers, and slammed into a cabinet door, cracking it. Lelani was already scratching and biting at the dazed feline, spitting out tufts of hair as she tore large avulsions in her hissing, scratching pet. She bit into Prince Charles's tender belly, unraveling his intestines and devouring them, slurping them up like linguini, burrowing up into the cat, chewing through the soft organs as blood poured over her face and the cat yowled and clawed her face. Without a thought, Lelani broke both of Prince Charles's front legs to prevent him from scratching her again. The limbs splintered and jagged shards of white bone ripped through the soft fur as she continued eating the agonized animal. She tore off his hind legs and gnawed them like chicken wings while the cat continued to hiss and howl. Its pain was unable to touch her humanity, obscured beneath a tenebrous veil of desperate appetite.

**2.**

BILL BUTLER walked off the plane wearing khaki cargo shorts, a deep-blue Ralph Lauren polo shirt, and a pair of brown John Lobb loafers. Even dressed casually, he looked like money. He smiled and winked at the young Asian flight attendant who'd served him throughout his flight. She was tiny, only about a hundred pounds, maybe less. She had long black hair that hung down to her waist and a smile that enveloped the entire cabin. She took Bill's hand, passing him her phone number.

"I hope you enjoyed your flight, sir. Come fly with us again soon," she said, smiling back at him and mouthing the words "call me."

Bill nodded. He felt so good he almost skipped down to baggage claim. There was nothing more invigorating than having his sex appeal validated by the attentions of a beautiful young woman.

He had just designed what was destined to be one of the hottest video games around based on a popular movie in which the world is overrun by vampires. The project had been green-lighted, with a budget of more than one hundred million. He was dating two models with the recent prospect of adding a young, hot, Asian stewardess... uh... flight attendant to the stable. He had just bought a new Mercedes, his first, and he was having a new house built in downtown Austin, right off Congress Avenue, with a price tag of more than seven hundred thousand. He was the very definition of success, and he was only thirty years old.

Bill retrieved his luggage and made his way to long-term parking. He couldn't wait to see his new baby. He'd just purchased it when he'd been called away to Los Angeles to finalize the deal for the new video game. He'd only driven it two or three times. The reality that he actually owned a goddamn Mercedes was still sinking in.

It took Bill several breathless minutes wandering around the airport parking lot before he spotted his baby, a ninety-four thousand dollar high-gloss, metallic-black, six-cylinder 2013 Mercedes Benz S-class. Bill smiled and unlocked the doors, popped the trunk, and started the engine with his remote. He tossed his Samsonite carry-on and garment bag into the trunk and slipped behind the wheel. Bill turned up the radio and gunned the engine like a teenager with his first car.

The drive to the condo was too brief. Bill hardly had time to open the engine up before he was pulling into the building's underground parking garage. He turned off his Android phone and tucked it in the glove compartment beneath his registration and insurance papers, and then turned on his iPhone and checked his messages. Lelani didn't know about the Android phone. That one was for the six-foot blonde Scandinavian woman he'd met at a fashion show in Holland last year. Her name was Suzanna and she was a twenty-three-year-old up-and-coming fashion model, thirteen years younger than Lelani. He had a separate e-mail account just for her and an apartment in Houston where he'd meet her whenever she was in town. By all accounts, Bill was the mutherfucking man. He had everything a man could want times two. He couldn't wipe the smile from his face as he locked the Mercedes and set the alarm.

Bill smiled at a young couple he'd seen coming in and out of the building several times. The guy was young and cocky. A six-foot, blond-haired, blue-eyed pretty boy who probably lived off his daddy's trust fund. His bleach-blonde girlfriend looked like the typical club-hopping speed-freak or coke-whore with an IQ lower than her number of sexual partners. Bill winked at her as he walked to the elevator and she smiled and waved, eliciting a stern look along with a sneer complete with puffed-out chest from her boyfriend. Bill held his hands up in surrender and smiled wider as the elevator doors closed. He pushed the button for the penthouse, whistling a tune from an old hip-hop song, something about pimping big and spending cheese.

He always heard hip-hop or heavy metal lyrics in his head when he felt like this. His hubris had its own soundtrack. He had a play list on his iPod full of songs by Jay-Z, Will Smith, Lil Wayne, and Kanye West interspersed with Led Zeppelin, Guns N' Roses, Motley Crew, and Van Halen for when he needed to pump himself up or when his ego was already on full blast and he wanted to continue stoking the fire. Today, he felt truly gangsta, like the mutherfucking pimp of the year—the white-bread yuppie version at least.

The elevator doors opened, and Bill pulled out his keys and walked across the hall to his front door. He unlocked and opened the door with a flourish. The powerful stench of body odor, rotting food, and fetid blood and meat immediately assailed his nostrils. He recoiled and covered his nose with his forearm. "Jesus! What the fuck? Lelani!"

The instant he spoke her name, a feeling of dread crushed down upon him.

"Lelani?" he whispered, taking a few tentative steps into the condominium, leaving the door open in case he needed to make a hasty retreat, and cueing up 911 on his cell phone. He'd seen too many horror movies and episodes of *Law and Order* to take any chances. It smelled like something had died and then something else had eaten its putrid carcass and regurgitated it.

Lelani wasn't answering. That just couldn't be good. Now Bill wished he'd gotten his concealed-weapons permit. He owned two guns, a Glock 9mm and a Desert Eagle .45. Both were in the closet in the master bedroom and hadn't been fired since the first month he'd owned them.

The apartment was dark. Bill groped for the light switch in a near panic. His imagination was working overtime, and he kept anticipating the touch of a cold, dead hand on his own. Chills raced along his spine before he found the switch and the light chased back the night, but not the dread or the feeling that something wasn't right. If anything, seeing the chaos of the penthouse—the smears of food on the counters, walls, and floors, the empty food cartons and containers, broken plates, jars, and bottles—increased his anxiety.

Then he saw the blood. A long streak led from the kitchen to the living room. It didn't appear to be a fatal amount, but Bill had no idea how much blood leaked out of a human body. His finger hovered over the call button on his iPhone as he followed the trail of gore. When he spotted the pile of splintered cat bones, a small, blue collar festooned with rhinestones and affixed with a crown-shaped tag strewn among the remains, a sob choked in Bill's throat.

"P-Prince Charles?"

Bill's bottom lip trembled and his voice cracked with emotion. The bones had been flensed of flesh and gnawed on, cracked open, and the marrow sucked out. Even the skull had been broken open and plundered, the brain pan licked clean. Bill looked back at the open front door. His legs trembled.

"Lelani? Are you here? You okay?"

Bill walked farther into the apartment. His curiosity gradually overcame his caution even as his imagination terrorized him with images of Lelani in varying states of dismemberment, posed in garish, nightmarish positions culled from every slasher movie he'd ever seen.

He rushed into the kitchen to arm himself with one of the Gunter Wilhelm carving knives from the cutlery set on his counter before finishing his search of the apartment. On the kitchen counter he found Lelani, crouched like a cat right next to the seven hundred dollar knife set he'd bought on an impulse, determined to become a master chef after watching a particularly rousing episode of *Hell's Kitchen*. She looked like hell. Her hair looked like she'd been plugged into a Tesla coil. Her eyes were wild, pupils dilated to the size of nickels, and her face was smeared with blood and tufts of gray fur. More than that, she was drawn and withered, like an old woman. Her eyes were hollow pits, her cheeks sunken in.

"Lelani? Why didn't you answer me? What the hell did you do to my cat?" Anger grew inside him, masking the fear temporarily but not displacing it. His legs still trembled and the hair on the back of his neck stood on end. The persistence of his paranoia only increased his anger.

"Answer me, Lelani! What the fuck is wrong with you? Are you high again?"

Lelani growled and bared canines that were clearly larger than they should have been, longer, sharper, and tipped with red. Bill took a step back. The dozens of vampire movies he'd watched in his lifetime came flooding back. Feeling ridiculous, he dropped his Smartphone, crossed his fingers, and began backing away from her, looking around for something wooden to use as a stake. The table and chairs were made of stainless steel. No luck there.

Lelani slithered down off the countertop on all fours, sniffing the air and licking her lips. Her eyes were blood-red and smoldering with lust, but not the type of lust Bill was accustomed to seeing in the eyes of women. There was nothing sexual in it. Nothing in her eyes showed any awareness of his humanity or personhood. It was worse than the physical objectification he'd often been accused of when he looked at women, reducing them to mere breasts, asses, and pretty faces.

But her stare didn't reduce him to a collection of body parts. It reduced him to mere meat. It was the way poor kids in the ghetto salivated over McDonald's cheeseburgers. And Lelani was salivating. Her mouth hung open. Those queer, red-tipped fangs glistened in the light. Thick ropes of saliva, tinged pink with old blood, drooled from each corner of her mouth.

"Lelani? It's me, Bill. What's wrong with you?"

She growled at the sound of his voice and scurried across the floor toward him. Bill leaped backward. His back slammed against the open refrigerator door. Whatever was wrong with her had eaten away at her, reducing her to skin and bones. She looked like a fucking Holocaust victim. A hoarse gravely voice, so unlike the dulcet, Marilyn Monroe-esque purr Lelani normally affected, scratched its way out of her larynx.

"Hungry, Bill. I'm so hungry." Her eyes didn't meet his when she spoke. Instead they roamed his body from head to toe, sizing him up.

"Okay. Okay. Let me—let me get you something to eat, sweetheart." Bill put on his best lady-killer smile, but terror leeched all conviction from the expression.

Lelani shook her head. "Noooooo time. Hungry now!" She crooned in a raspy, graveyard howl. Her voice sounded like what you'd imagine a mummy's voice would sound like after a thousand years in a crypt, but it had been only a few days since he'd seen her last. There was no sane explanation for her radical transformation except…

"You're a vampire, right? No, it's okay. I understand. That's it, isn't it? Someone bit you? You got bit by a vampire and now you're one too, right? You need blood, right? I can get you blood. I can get all the blood you want. There's a whole nightclub on Sixth Street full of kids who'd gladly let you suck their blood. Those wannabes would go fucking nuts over a real-life vampire," Bill said, nodding vigorously in a failed attempt to solicit Lelani's assent.

Lelani stalked closer, so close Bill could smell the overwhelming bestial stench of her, a suffocating miasma of sweat, bad breath, and rot. Bill scowled in disgust and covered his face with his forearm. Lelani seized the arm and savagely bit into it, ripping a huge chunk of muscle and tendon down to the bone. The pink flesh of Bill's forearm stretched like taffy before tearing away from the ulna. Naked bone streaked with red showed through the ragged avulsion.

Bill screamed, a shrill, high-pitched cry. With his free hand, he made a fist and punched Lelani as hard as he could. She staggered backward, and Bill kicked her in the chest, putting his hips into it as if he was kicking down a door, sending Lelani sprawling across the garbage-strewn floor.

She lay there, still chewing the hunk of meat she'd ripped from Bill's arm. Then she swallowed the raw flesh, licked blood and skin from her lips, and wiped her face with her own forearm. She smiled joyously, like a kid eating an ice cream cone, revealing those bizarre fangs that were now stained with Bill's blood. Bill turned and ran.

He hurtled Lelani's prone form and charged for the door, screaming, "Heeeeelp! *Help!* HEEEEEEELP!!!"

He didn't make it far. The bite on his forearm had transferred a powerful neurotoxin into his bloodstream. His thundering heartbeat quickly spread the venom throughout his body, causing painful cramps in his muscles. He fell to the ground, doubled over in agony. It felt as if every muscle in his body had a Charlie horse. He tried to crawl the rest of the way out of the room. Tiny hands clamped down on his ankles like vices. Bill had never realized before how small Lelani's hands were. With strength he never knew she possessed, Lelani dragged him back into the apartment and slammed the door.

Her beady bloodshot eyes fixed on his legs. Without hesitation, Lelani seized his thigh in both hands and sank her canines deep into the muscle.

"No! Get off me! Get the fuck off me!"

Bill punched at her, but his arms felt weak. Whatever had caused the painful muscle spasms had also robbed him of his strength.

Lelani's jaws locked tight on his thigh, and she chewed on him like a wolf gnawing at a deer. She jerked her head sideways in a sudden violent motion, jerking the muscle free, peeling it away from the bone with a wet, sticky, ripping sound that made Bill think of peeling a mango. The pain was nauseating. His stomach rolled and threatened to revolt as waves of anguish singed his senses.

As he helplessly watched, she wrenched the muscle from its moorings and swallowed the bleeding meat in huge gulps. The room swam and everything turned gray, swirling like an amusement park ride before darkness overtook him.

><

BILL regained consciousness in blinding, white-hot agony. He looked down at his leg and saw bone. The area from his thigh down had been completely stripped of muscle, fat, and sinew.

"*Oh my God! You ate my fucking leg!* HEEEEEELLLP! *My fucking leg! Somebody help me!*"

Beside him, Lelani lay in a puddle of Bill's blood. Her face was a fright-mask of gore. She stirred at the sound of his voice, lifting herself to a sitting position and sniffing the air, looking around with her beady, blood-shot eyes. Her gaze fell on Bill's remaining leg, and something like a smile—but less jovial, more carnivorous—crossed her face. Her lips, teeth, and tongue were stained a ghastly wine color, coated with blood and bits of flesh. She chewed some leftover piece of gristle, fat, or tendon from Bill's cannibalized limb. Ropes of bloody drool spilled from the corners of her mouth onto the floor. She wiped her lips with her forearm again and sniffed the air once more, again catching Bill's scent. Her eyes closed and her smile widened. She looked like she'd just taken a hit of some really good shit and was pausing to savor the rush. When she opened her eyes and locked them once again on Bill, they were aflame with a ravenous, predatory lust.

Bill screamed and tried to crawl away from her as she rushed over to him and seized his remaining leg.

"No! Oh, God, No! Don't! Please stop! Heeeelp!!! Oh God, noooooooo!"

With ferocious savagery, using only her teeth and fingernails, Lelani ripped large chunks of meat from Bill's remaining leg. He punched and struck at her with his diminished strength but was unable to dislodge her from his leg. He was so weak; he felt like he was swimming through tar. The aftereffects of her apparently venomous saliva, hypovolemic shock, and the excruciating pain and horror of being eaten alive threatened to render him unconscious again. He fought as hard to hold onto consciousness as he did to get Lelani off him. Both were losing battles.

Lelani didn't stop at his legs. Bill called out to every god he'd ever heard of, praying for Jesus or Krishna or Buddha or Allah to take him away from this horror as she progressed up his thighs, ripping away his khaki shorts and tearing off his penis in one quick violent motion. Bill screamed again, and now his prayers changed from pleas for salvation and rescue to desperate entreaties for a quick death or at least unconsciousness so he wouldn't feel what was to come. She chewed sloppily, dropping bits of Bill's sexual organ onto the floor and then scooping them up and cramming the bloody scraps of cock-flesh back into her mouth and gulping them down. Blood, urine, and semen spattering the floor, leaked from the hideous gash where his sex had been. That's when Bill finally lost consciousness.

He dreamt of cruising Sixth Street for low-mileage club sluts behind the wheel of his new Mercedes on a Saturday night, waving to the gaggles of drunken, giggling, Sixth Street skanks staggering out of the bars in tight-fitting miniskirts and baby T-shirts sans brassiere, nipples jabbing their way through the thin cotton fabric, tight, flat stomachs peeking out seductively from beneath their shirts. He saw himself offering them a ride in his ninety thousand dollar bitch-magnet and ending the evening getting head in a parking lot.

He reawakened to the reality of the bleeding wound where his cock had been and screamed himself unconscious again. He woke two more times. Each time there was more of him missing until he'd lost so much blood that his heart sputtered and stopped.

LELANI continued to feast, glutting herself on her lecherous fiancée. In death, he satisfied her far more than he ever had in life. Finally, his commitment to her was total, absolute. No other woman would ever come between them again. They were now united forever—or at least until her next bowel movement.

**3.** **T**HE KIDS were crying and screaming and yelling and begging and just being the fucking brats their mother had raised them to be by failing to raise them at all. Kitty, Kelly, and little Nathan Gingred Jr. had been relegated to a succession of nannies for as long as he could remember. Lillian (Mrs. Nathan Gingred) spent her time at cocktail parties, the yoga studio, Pilates studio, some charity function or another, or shopping, always shopping. Her only contribution to child raising was buying the kids whatever their spoiled little hearts desired and hiring a new nanny whenever the old one got fed up and quit. When she wasn't around, they bugged him for shit, and Nathan could not take that right now. The last thing he needed was to hear them whine about going out for ice cream or hamburgers or to some store to buy some stupid toy or go to some ridiculous amusement park or buy some mindless videogame. He just didn't need that shit. The baby crying was bad enough without the twins adding to the cacophony with their pealing cries for attention.

"Daddyyyyyyyyy! We're booooooored!"

"We want some ice creeeeeeeam!"

"We're huuuUUUNGRYYYYYY!"

What the fuck do they know about being hungry? Nathan felt like he'd just emerged from a month-long trek across the Mojave desert. He'd just eaten an hour ago, but it felt like he'd been on a hunger strike for weeks. He just couldn't seem to get enough food. He'd had his personal chef on 'round-the-clock duty since he'd come back from the clinic, since he'd gotten the treatment. He'd ordered all his favorite foods—twice—and then he'd begun organizing anything and everything in the pantry. The pantry was the size of a studio apartment, and he'd emptied it in three days. Now he had to wait while Philippe replenished it. The man had been gone for more than two hours, and Nathan was growing increasingly impatient and irritable and downright fucking mean.

"*Shut the fuck up!*" It wasn't the first time he'd yelled at his kids. He'd even taken a hand to them more than once. He didn't buy all that touchy-feely liberal bullshit about not beating your kids when they got out of line. If he didn't work so much and had more time to spend with his kids, he'd have gotten them in line by now. Damn straight. Let those fucking hippies raise their kids to be disrespectful little fuckers if they wanted to. His kids went to church and had learned to fear the Lord, and more importantly, they had learned to fear Daddy. But his failed campaign for the presidency had kept him away from the house, on and off, for more than a year. In that time, he'd lost control of the household somehow and his kids had turned into little assholes.

"But we're booooored and we're huuuuuuungry! You ate everything!"

"One more word and I'm coming out there with the belt!" Nathan called from his study. The kids were playing right outside his door. Thirteen bedrooms, a twenty-foot by thirty-foot playroom filled with every toy known to man, a media room with theater seating for twenty and a screen the size of a small Cineplex stocked with hundreds of DVDs, an Olympic-sized swimming pool, and six acres of rolling green landscape to play in, yet they chose to camp out right outside his fucking door. *Jesus Christ!*

From the nursery, little Nathaniel Jr. was doing his best Aretha Franklin impersonation, crying out at the top of his infant lungs.

The nanny was off today, and his wife was at a charity function in Manhattan, which left Nathan to deal with it. He pushed himself away from his massive oak desk, noting with no small amount of satisfaction how close he was able to sit by the desk now that his belly was gone.

"I'm coming, damnit!" He stormed over to the locked study door. He turned the latch and swung it open. The twins were waiting for him. Identical pigtails and pinched, agonized expressions greeted him. They had their arms crossed and were looking at him expectantly, as if he was late for an appointment.

"Are we going, Daddy?"

"We're not going anywhere. I'm going to change your brother." He pushed past his two daughters and headed for the stairs.

"Mommy said for you to take us to Tally's for lunch."

"Mommy isn't here."

"We called her and she said you'd take us," the twins crooned in unison as they followed their irritated father up the staircase.

Nathan whirled on them, snarling ferociously. "And I said Mommy isn't here and we're not going anywhere! Philippe will be back with the food any minute."

Truth be told, the idea of going out for a hot meal sounded perfect right now. Except Tally's was one of the most popular restaurants in New Jersey and was always packed, and the drive to the boardwalk was nearly ten miles. It would take them half an hour to get ready, another twenty minutes to drive there, and then at least another twenty minutes before the first miniscule appetizers were brought out, which would do nothing but tease Nathan's voracious appetite. It could be as long as two hours from the house to a hot entree. Philippe, on the other hand, could be back any minute with a van full of groceries, and he could whip up something quick for them to eat while they waited for the main course.

"We want Tally's!"

"*I said no!*" Nathan struck both of them with one sweep of his hand, slapping one jaw and then the next and sending them both stumbling backward down the stairs with stunned expressions on their faces. He didn't even look back as he stomped up the stairs to Junior's room.

"I'm telling Mommy!" he heard behind him. It took a heroic effort for Nathan not to run back down the stairs and beat both his daughters within an inch of their lives.

Upstairs, the baby was going into hysterics. Junior's screams had become increasingly histrionic. It sounded like he was being tortured. He was just spoiled and impatient like the rest of Nathan's kids. *And why the fuck do I have to deal with them? Why isn't Lillian here? Why isn't the goddamn nanny dealing with this bullshit?* Nathan's patience imploded. It was like a star collapsing in on itself and forming a black hole. And that black hole was right in the pit of Nathan's stomach. He was so hungry he could barely see straight, and Junior's cries were like knife blades lancing through his skull. At that moment, he completely understood mothers who drowned their babies.

His blood pressure was boiling when Nathan slammed open the door to the nursery and spotted the shrieking, crying, urine-soaked thing in the Eddie Bauer designer crib. Nathan was rougher than he meant to be when he snatched the hysterical little creature from the hand-loomed, six hundred-thread-count Egyptian cotton sheets. He dropped little Nathaniel onto the changing table, eliciting even louder shrieks. Nathan grit his teeth and balled up his fists. Every muscle contracted with the effort to control his increasing tension and frustration, to quell the feral rage building up inside him. His stomach rumbled, and he nearly swooned from both the hunger and the splitting migraine he had as a result of it, made worse by the shrieking thing with the diaper that seemed to hold half the child's weight in urine. Nathan pulled off the diaper, tossed it into the Diaper Genie, wiped Junior down with scented wipes, powdered his bottom, and slipped on a fresh diaper. He did it expertly, as if he'd done it every day of his life. The twins had made him deft at all things baby, and even though he didn't spend half as much time with Junior as he had with them, he hadn't lost the knack. But the kid was still screaming.

In addition to all the food in the pantry, Nathan had drank all the breast milk Lillian pumped before taking off for Manhattan. There was nothing for Junior to eat until Philippe came back. Nathan plopped a pacifier in the baby's mouth. A few desperate sucks and a brief moment of silence and then Nathan laid his son back in his crib, and the boy spit out his pacifier and began wailing again. Nathan clamped his hands over his ears. His head felt like it had been struck with an axe, and the hunger was so much worse now. He shoved the pacifier back in Junior's mouth. He sucked it twice and spit it out again. Nathan repeated the motion two more times, pacifier in, pacifier out, before giving up and clamping a hand over Junior's mouth to silence him.

"Shut. Up."

His hand covered the boy's entire face, mouth, nose, and eyes. It wasn't long before the boy fell silent. Nathan panicked. He lifted his son to his face to be sure he was still breathing. He listened for a heartbeat. It was there, steady and strong. The boy had merely passed out from lack of oxygen, but he would be fine. Nathan smelled him. He smelled so much better now that his diaper had been changed, like baby powder and that fresh, doughy, new-baby smell that reminded Nathan of fresh-baked bread. Nathan's mouth began to water—and then he bit Junior's arm.

He did it without thinking, sucking his son's chubby little arm into his mouth and biting down. The boy woke up screaming, and Nathan clamped a hand over the boy's face again. This time he held it there long after the boy had fallen silent again. He removed his hand and put his ear to Junior's chest. He could no longer hear his son's heartbeat. All Nathan was aware of was that wonderful new-baby smell and that soft, supple, new-baby skin, and that tender, succulent, new-baby meat that seemed to melt in his mouth with each bite. It was like eating an apple, a juicy living apple with dimples and eyes just like Nathan's.

ON A soundstage in Studio City, preparations were underway for another evening of live entertainment. It was the most popular show on television. Young vocalists lined up outside the studio for hours, hoping for their shot at instant stardom. The three celebrity hosts were Lionel Douglas, a young record producer from London who'd been responsible for some of the biggest musical acts of the nineties; Diane Taylor, an overmedicated pop vocalist from the late-eighties/ early nineties; and Samuel "Big Easy" Saldeine, one of the hottest and most sought-after music producers in the business.

Big Easy had made millions producing top-forty hits for some of the biggest names in the music industry. He'd been the man behind the scenes for pop and R&B divas, hip-hop moguls, and rock superstars. Now he was center stage, and all eyes were about to be on him and his two co-hosts. That's why he'd gone to the Aphrodite Aesthetic Reconstruction Clinic for their latest miracle weight-loss cure. He'd lost more than ninety pounds since the treatment and was now down to a svelte one hundred eighty pounds at six-foot-four—and he was starving. He'd been eating without relent since the treatment. His dressing room was littered with the remains of fruit and cold-cut trays, the carcasses of turkeys, chickens, and various fish, along with bones from random cow and hog parts.

"Hey! Big Easy! You ready for this?" asked the annoyingly ebullient producer/ director with the dyed blond quaff and gloriously white capped-teeth.

"Let's just get this shit started. I'm fucking starving!" he growled. Ever since the treatment, since the hunger had come on like the apocalypse, his temper had grown shorter. He'd yelled at waiters, argued with room service, threatened the pizza delivery man, and almost made one of the caterers cry this morning when she'd run out of meat. It wasn't lost on him that all the incidents had involved food.

"Really? I heard catering just sent a full stuffed turkey to your dressing room a couple hours ago. You didn't eat?" the producer asked.

"Yeah, I ate it. Now I'm hungry again. What the fuck does it matter to you? Just get this shit going so I can get to dinner!"

The producer raised an eyebrow and snickered. "A whole turkey? And that wasn't dinner?"

Big Easy lost his trademark even temper. He rose from his chair and stormed over to the producer, seconds before the show was supposed to go live. His co-hosts had just taken their places on stage and were staring at him like he'd lost his mind. He wasn't sure he hadn't. All he could think about was eating, and anything that came between him and his next meal was his mortal enemy. Right now, that was the hyperactive producer with the Colgate smile.

"What are you doing? We're live in thirty seconds!"

"Are you calling me greedy? Is that it? I've got a thyroid problem. I'm not fucking greedy! You think I'm fuckin' fat, you snotty sonofabitch!"

The producer raised his hands and took a few steps back, smiling and chuckling, still seemingly unconcerned with the angry, six-foot-four-inch man charging toward him.

"Whoa! Whoa! We're cool, man. We're cool. You are trippin', Easy." He shook his head and snickered again. That was what finally pushed Big Easy over the edge. He balled up his fists.

"Are you laughing at me, motherfucka?"

"I'm just sayin', you're talkin' like you still weigh three-hundred pounds. Have you looked at yourself lately? Whatever you're doing, exercise, meth, crack, that shit is workin'. So lighten the hell up, dude. Don't go all ghetto on me now. We've got ten seconds to air."

"Don't tell me to fuckin' lighten up, motherfucka! You wanna see ghetto? I'll show your bitch-ass ghetto!"

The first punch landed flush on the left side of the producer's porcelain chin, dropping him to his knees and making the room spin. He held his hands out in front of him, trying to ward off the still-advancing, still-murderously angry music producer.

"What the fuck, Easy? You fucking hit me!"

Easy growled, revealing his elongated red-tipped canines. The producer's eyes widened, and he let out a tiny yelp and a squeak like a kicked cat. The next punch dropped him face first onto the floor, where Easy began to stomp and kick him in the side of the head. His Bruno Magli loafers cut the producer's scalp and drew blood. The next kick turned the gash into a yawning maw.

"Easy! Jesus Christ, *stop!*" someone yelled.

Easy didn't know who and didn't care. The hunger had made him insane, enraged, and venting that rage on the producer's skull felt amazing. The producer rolled onto his back and with his arms tried to shield his face from Easy's blows. Someone grabbed Easy's right arm and, Easy gave the guy a left hook for his troubles. A security guard grabbed him by both arms and tried to pull his arms behind his back. Another guard tried to slip an arm around Easy's throat. Easy bit the second rent-a-cop's hand, crushing bones and snapping fingers. A finger came off in his mouth and Easy instinctively chewed it up and swallowed it. The guard screamed and pulled away. He collapsed to his knees, holding his bleeding hand, and then rolled over onto his back and began to convulse as the neurotoxin in Easy's saliva invaded his bloodstream and caused his muscles to seize.

The other guard pulled away too, holding his hands palms up in surrender, terrified and paid far too little to risk getting torn apart by a guy with fangs like a damn vampire. Easy turned back to the producer, who was trying to climb to his feet. He leaped onto the man's back, driving him back down to the floor where Easy began to bite him, ripping chunks from the producer's arms, tearing down to the bone as the man screamed and begged, and a viewing audience of thirty million watched in horror.

 **5.**

66"WHAT THE fuck did you do to my client?" Dr. David Ebersol asked, wiping his shoulder-length mane of frizzy, unwashed blond hair back out of his face and rubbing the bald spot at the center of it in the same unconscious motion. He was not a small man at six feet two and just over two hundred pounds. He looked farm-boy strong, a combination of muscle and fat. He gave the appearance of one who'd never spent a day in the gym but had acquired muscle through hard work.

Dr. Trevor Adams, in contrast, spent every day in the gym, working hard on his chiseled physique, but he was a naturally smaller man, just five seven and 175 pounds. Ebersol had seen the young molecular biologist gain 40 pounds of muscle in the six or seven months he'd known the man. He suspected Dr. Adams had been self-subscribing and administering genetic hormone boosters. The same brand of gene-therapy he'd no doubt given his client, but with very different results.

"What are you talking about?" Dr. Ebersol was red in the face and breathing hard like he'd just run sprints.

"Lelani Simms. What the fuck did you do to her?"

"The model? She wanted to lose weight without going on a diet or spending hours in the gym. That's what they all want. Her exact words to me were, 'I want to be able to eat whatever the hell I want and not gain a pound.' So I helped her out."

"You-you, what? You injected her with some kind of DNA or something?"

Trevor Adams raised an eyebrow and squinted at Dr. Ebersol. "Why are you asking me this?"

"I've been getting calls from her for the last three days, ever since she left here. She said she can't stop eating and she was losing weight like crazy. I referred her to you, so I want to know what the fuck you did to her."

Trevor shrugged. "I don't understand. What's the problem? Sounds like she got exactly what she asked for."

Dr. Ebersol lunged forward and Trevor winced. Even with his new muscle and size, he still felt like the little guy, especially around naturally large men like Ebersol.

Dr. Trevor Adams wasn't just the smaller man, he was younger by almost two decades. He'd graduated from Stanford University with a doctorate degree at the remarkable age of twenty two. He was a genius, a prodigy. The only reason he was working for the clinic instead of at some prestigious think tank was because of a few ethical lapses early in his young career.

He was still in college when he was implicated in a gene-doping scandal involving an Olympic powerlifter and an artificial genetic retro-virus called Repoxygen. He'd allegedly used the virus to transport a gene for the production of myostatin and insulin-like growth factor I, which affects muscle production, and peroxisome proliferator-activated receptors, a family of proteins that regulate metabolism. The treatment failed, and the Olympian developed leukemia and died. Text messages between Trevor and the powerlifter cast suspicion on him, but no conclusive evidence could be found. After graduation, the young biologist was again embroiled in a controversy, this time involving Olympic sprinters.

A German track coach had allegedly contacted him about procuring Repoxygen, and using it to insert a gene for erythropoietin, a hormone that tells the body to make more red blood cells, which carry oxygen to muscles. The Olympic committee believed he had planned to use it to increase his athlete's endurance. There were also e-mails between the two regarding injecting "naked" DNA directly into athletes' muscles to permanently alter their genes and make them more muscular through the release of growth hormones. The e-mails suggested that some athletes had already been injected but that their immune systems had fought off the foreign genetic material. Both Trevor and the track coach were permanently banned from any association with the Olympics and Olympic competitors, and any athletes found associating with either man would likewise be permanently banned from Olympic competition. It was soon after that that Dr. Trevor Adams was contacted by the Aphrodite Aesthetic Reconstruction Clinic.

"She can't stop eating! That's the fucking problem! She says she can't sleep, can't work, all she can think about is eating. Her metabolism is completely screwed up! What the hell did you give her?"

"I tried something new. I perfected the use of Repoxygen to transport DNA and transfer genetic traits from one host to another. It's been a huge success. I'm booked up for the rest of the year."

"What kind of genetic material are you using?"

"Pygmy shrew DNA."

"What?"

"I isolated the gene that controls the pygmy shrew's metabolism. Did you know they have one of the fastest metabolisms of any animal on the planet? They don't even store fat cells."

Dr. Ebersol's fingers clenched and unclenched, making a white-knuckled fist and then relaxing as if he couldn't decide if he wanted to punch Trevor in the face or strangle the life out of him.

Trevor's eyes watered, anticipating a beating.

"Well, did *you* know that because they don't store fat, they have to eat every two fucking hours or they'll die? They eat twice their body weight every day. They kill animals twice their size. They are some of the most vicious animals on the planet because they are always hungry! And you put those traits in a fucking human being! Are you crazy?"

Trevor held up his hands. "Whoa! Whoa, David! I'm sure it's not as bad as you're making it out to be. I've seen about a dozen patients so far this week, and I haven't heard any complaints. Why don't you try calling her again? I'm sure she's fine."

Ebersol reached into his pocket for his cell phone. He pointed a finger at Trevor like he was aiming a gun. "You stay right the fuck there!"

Trevor raised his hands. "I'm not going anywhere."

The phone rang for a long time before someone finally answered. "Hello? Lelani?"

A low growl came from the phone.

"Lelani? It's me, David. Dr. Ebersol."

A howl erupted from the phone, filled with pain and rage. It seemed to go on forever, increasing in volume until it became an ear-piercing scream. Both doctors trembled as they listened.

"Lelani? What's wrong? What's wrong?"

"I'm so, hungry! Hungry! HUUUUUUNGRYYYYYY!!!"

"Do you have anything there to eat? I'm catching a flight back to Austin. I'll be there soon. You just need to keep your nourishment up until I get there. Is there any food in the house?"

"Bill."

"Bill's there? Can he go get you some food?"

"No."

"Why not? Put him on the phone?"

"I ate him."

"What did you say?"

"I ate Bill. I'm so hungry. Help me! Help me! I'm SO HUNGRY!"

Dr. Ebersol hung up. All the blood had drained from his face. He looked visibly shaken.

"What? What did she say?"

Dr. Ebersol punched the young biologist, smashing his nose and depositing him on his ass.

"Jesus Christ! You broke my fucking nose! I'm calling the police! I'm going to sue you for everything you own or will ever own! Fuck, man! Are you crazy?"

"Am I crazy? You have the fucking nerve to ask me if I'm crazy? You want to know what she said? She ate her fucking fiancé. That's what she said. She ate her fucking fiancé! You reckless fucking asshole!"

"Oh, shit," Trevor said. He stopped wiping the blood from his nose and just sat there on the floor with his mouth hanging open, staring straight ahead with a glazed expression on his face.

"What—what do we do?"

"We? I should let your ass go down for this, but you'd take the whole clinic down with you. We'll ask Sarai. But we need to do some damage control in the meantime. Go wash your fucking face. And don't worry about your nose. I'll have Jim fix it later. It was too fucking big anyway. You look like Henry Winkler. Tell him to give you something that won't break as easily. I have a feeling I'm going to want to hit you again when I get back from Austin."

"You're really going there? I mean, she ate a dude."

"Look, you little piece of shit. I've known Lelani for more than ten years, ever since we started this clinic. She was one of our first clients. I'm more than just her dietician. I'm her fucking psychiatrist. She's been to my home, eaten with my family, played with my kids. I brought her to you because she was desperate and you were supposed to be some kind of genius."

"Look, I'm sorry, man. I fucked up."

Trevor held his hand out for Dr. Ebersol to help him up from the floor, and Ebersol smacked it away and hissed. Trevor scrambled to his feet and snatched a handful of cotton balls from a jar and shoved them up his nose to stop the bleeding.

"This shit you injected into my client, this retro-virus, is it contagious?"

"What?"

"Can it spread? I need to know how bad you've fucked up here. Is it communicable?"

"Repoxygen? No. It's not communicable."

"What if it mutates?"

"It's an engineered virus. It won't mutate."

"It won't or it can't?"

"It won't. I mean, I suppose it could. I didn't make the damn virus. I just used it to transport the DNA. I didn't invent the shit."

"So you don't really know if it could spread or not? You injected a dozen people with an untested genetic virus that you don't know shit about?"

"The virus has been tested. I didn't alter the virus. I just added the DNA to it."

"You'd better hope this shit you concocted doesn't cause any more damage than it already has."

Trevor's eyes widened and he put a hand over his mouth.

"Oh, shit."

"What?"

"The girl! The little girl!" Trevor began rifling through a stack of files on his desk.

"What girl? Don't tell me you injected that shit into a kid?"

"She was a teenager. Fifteen years old. Her parents brought her in because she was severely obese and none of the diets they tried were working. They even hired her a personal trainer. Nothing was working. She was being teased at school."

"So you thought it would be a good idea to fuck with her genes?"

"I thought it would be safe, and her parents were willing to pay anything for it. Sarai told them about it. They wanted it. They were insistent."

"Here it is. The girl's name is Star. Star Mourning."

"Star *Mourning*? You mean—? Ah, don't fucking tell me. Alexis and Mike Mourning, the actors, their daughter?"

"Yeah. I think so."

"Then we're fucked. The media will be all over us if she goes rabid like Lelani did, if they aren't already. After that, it's only a matter of time before the FDA comes beating on our door. They'll be lawsuits. Maybe even criminal charges."

Dr. Ebersol paced frantically, running his hands through his long, blond hair and rubbing the bald spot on top of his head.

"Not if we can get to them before the virus takes effect. I just injected her yesterday."

"Get us booked on the next flight back to the states. I need to get to Austin and you'd better get your ass to LA and see that kid."

6.

JAMIE AND Elaine could not remember when they weren't famous or weren't in love. They'd met on a children's TV show in the nineties. They'd were eleven and twelve years old when they fell in love. When the show ended, they both launched successful careers as pop singers, quickly becoming two of the biggest teen stars in the country. Their wedding was a national event. But age and the indulgences of wealth had taken their toll, and the media had not been kind.

A year ago, Elaine gave birth to their first child. Six months ago, she'd tried to make a comeback with a multimillion-dollar video and an appearance on a popular singing competition, but all anyone could talk about were her thick thighs, her paunch, and her "muffin top" bulging out over the top of her skin-tight jeans. Jamie had gained weight too, sympathy weight as he called it, and after seeing what his wife had gone through, he'd delayed his own reemergence into the spotlight. In truth, he'd become a recluse, hiding behind the walls of their multimillion-dollar estate. Rumors circulated that he'd put on hundreds of pounds and become some kind of obese shut-in. His agent urged him to show himself and dispel the rumors, but he was afraid. Then one day, his agent told him about the Aphrodite Aesthetic Reconstruction Clinic, and he'd made an appointment for him and his wife. The results were miraculous.

The two of them stood naked, admiring their new bodies. The treatment had been an amazing success. They looked as lean as they did when they'd scored their first top forty hit in 1995. Jamie even had a six pack. Jamie's trademark, ankle-length mane of raven-black hair had shocks of gray running through it now, but otherwise, he looked like a teenager again. And he was still losing weight. They both were.

Earlier that day, they'd made their first public appearance together since the birth of their new son. They had gone to the beach, and the paparazzi had followed like a pack of jackals, eager for shot of her bulging tummy or the coveted photo of Jamie's Hollywood physique turned Southern-fried fat. What they'd gotten instead were photos of the couple looking remarkably svelte, even a bit underweight. The couple had flaunted their new bodies in tiny bathing suits. She had worn a bikini so small it might as well have been made of dental floss.

"I'd have worn a Speedo, but that might have been a little too much," Jamie said.

"I think that would have been damn sexy," Elaine replied, kissing him on the neck with lips greasy with chicken fat.

They'd left the beach earlier than expected, both suddenly, urgently hungry. They went to a nearby restaurant and ordered small meals, appropriate for two megastars trying to maintain their celebrity waistlines. It hadn't touched their appetites, but the paparazzi was watching. They'd raced home, desperate for food.

"What the fuck is going on? I'm so hungry!"

Once home, they'd attacked their extensive pantry with maniacal fervor, eating everything they could get their hands on, shoving food into their mouths nonstop until the hunger finally abated.

"What's wrong with us?" Elaine asked.

"We're fine. It must just be some kind of side effect. The doctor said we could eat whatever we wanted. We probably just didn't eat enough at the restaurant."

Elaine smiled wanly, unconvinced.

They carried Gabrielle, their one-year-old son, up to his room and put him to bed. He'd been sitting in the pantry crying while they ignored him and ate and ate and ate. They felt guilty, but they were exhausted now. They laid him down with a warm bottle of breast milk. Then they retired to their room.

Jamie stripped off his board shorts and walked over to the mirror where Elaine joined him, sliding out of her bikini.

"It's amazing though, isn't it? We look like teenagers again."

"Except for the wrinkles," Elaine added, running her fingertips over the fine lines at the corner of his eye.

Jamie smiled. "Those just make us look wiser."

"Let's go lie down. I'm so tired."

They moved to the bed, but Jamie felt a stronger urge draw him, stronger than his need for sleep. He ran a hand over her naked backside and felt his manhood swell. He pressed his tumescent flesh against the cleft of Elaine's buttocks.

"Is that what I think it is? You can't be serious."

Elaine turned around, smiling devilishly and hugging her naked body to her husband, crushing his erection against her stomach. She reached between them and took his hard organ in hand, stroking it gently.

"We've been so busy, we haven't taken our new bodies for a test-drive yet. Let's make love. We can sleep after."

They kissed. It was a desperate, passionate kiss. Their tongues were at war between their joined lips. He sucked the air from her lungs as he crushed her body to his. Together they fell to the bed, lips, tongues, and writhing limbs intertwined like two clumsy teenagers racing toward ecstasy for the first time. He entered her from behind, grinding her face into the pillow as he thrust deep inside her. Elaine's body looked even slimmer now than it had just moments ago, as if she was losing weight minute by minute. He could see her ribcage through her back. Her vertebrae bulged through her skin, looking reptilian, like the bony plates on a dinosaur's back. He withdrew and rolled her over onto her back before entering her again in the missionary position. From the front, her weight loss was even more dramatic. Her breasts had shriveled like prunes. The nipples looked like two withered raisins. He could see every bone in her chest. Worst, he could feel himself getting hungry again.

They switched positions again. This time, Elaine was on top. Her skeletal face looked down at him, eyes gleaming with hunger and madness. He didn't remember her looking this emaciated earlier. It was as if their lovemaking was somehow accelerating her metabolism. Perhaps it was just because she was so small, only five feet, four inches tall and had weighed only 116 lbs when she'd weighed herself this morning. There had been so little nutrients left for her body to consume. Now it was apparently cannibalizing her muscle tissue.

Elaine smiled down at him. Her teeth looked all wrong, long and sharp and red. When she bit him, Jamie hardly noticed. He had already bitten off one of her breasts and was chewing it and swallowing it when she tore out his throat.

 **"MOM! I'M** hungry! I need something to eat!"

There were locks on the pantry door, the refrigerator, and even the cupboard where the coffee, tea, and spices were kept. Star Mourning tugged at the refrigerator door with all her might, muscles straining, sweat and tears bulleting down her face.

"I'm starving!"

"Don't be silly. You just ate. You're just being greedy. How do you expect to lose weight if you keep eating everything?"

"But I *am* losing weight! Look at me!" Star was about five feet, five inches tall and had weighed more than two hundred fifty pounds before her parents took her to the Aphrodite Aesthetic Reconstruction Clinic. On the drive to the airport, her mom had described some of the services they performed at the clinic: lap-band surgery, liposuction, wiring your jaw shut, feeding you through IV tubes, extreme exercise and diet programs, and plastic surgery. To Star, it had sounded like a house of horrors.

She was terrified and had cried during the entire drive to the airport. On the plane to Cancun, Star wept silently and refused to eat. Then, when they arrived at the clinic after a half-hour taxi ride and twenty minutes on a ferry, they sat with Dr. Sarai Mahendru, a tall, slender, Persian woman with long black hair, a perfect nose, big perky breasts she had obviously not been born with, and cat-like, multifaceted almond eyes.

"We have a new procedure one of our doctors has just developed that may be of interest to you. It's expensive, but it's permanent and only requires a single treatment."

"What's the treatment?" Star asked.

"If it works, we'll take it," her mother interrupted. Star cast a disapproving look at her mother, who crushed it in her own baleful gaze.

"The treatment involves gene modification. Basically, we alter your genes so they tell your body to stop producing fat cells."

"And how do you do that?"

"Recombinant DNA. We inject the new DNA directly into your bloodstream via a genetic retrovirus."

"A virus? I don't want a virus! No way!"

"It's completely safe. The virus is just used to spread the new DNA through your system. It's a transport system. It's completely harmless," the doctor said, smiling wide. Her teeth were perfectly straight and brilliantly white. Star suspected they were all either caps or dental implants. Most likely a combination of the two. The woman probably bleached her asshole and likely had had cosmetic surgery on her vagina so the labia were neat and trimmed and tucked perfectly inside her Brazilian-waxed clam. Star giggled and shook her head at the absurdity of the beauty-obsessed woman.

From the corner of her eye, she saw her mother's tanned complexion redden, her jaws tighten, and her nostrils flare.

"Enough! No more argument. The doctor says it works. You're getting it. Or do you want to stay fat forever?"

Star looked away from her mother, wiping a tear from her eye. She lowered her head and fell silent.

Alexis Mourning was an intimidating woman even to those she had not given birth to. She was more than an actress, she was a film icon who had starred in some of the most awarded and celebrated Hollywood productions of the last two decades. She was also stunningly beautiful. At forty-five, with the lithe, toned physique of a teenaged ballerina, she was the envy of women half her age. She had no wrinkles, no age spots or blemishes, and not an ounce of excess adipose tissue. Even the few wisps of gray in her raven-black hair made her look somehow more elegant, and she was universally praised for not coloring it. Her eyes were the type of blue poets wrote sonnets about, and her lips were perfectly bee-stung. What few outside the immediate family knew was that almost none of it was real. She starved herself, worked out like a madwoman, and regurgitated whatever extra calories she allowed herself to indulge in. When that didn't work, she rushed off to the plastic surgeon for some liposuction or spent an extended weekend being fed through IV tubes.

Her breasts were silicone bags molded by the skilled surgeons at the Aphrodite Clinic to have just the right amount of bounce and sag. It was enough to fool the most keen observer into believing they were real, but the greatest work of art was her face.

Alexis Mourning's ageless, wrinkle-free face was a tapestry of strategically placed surgical scars. Most were hidden along her hairline; the other faint, trace scars were masked behind a layer of custom designer makeup engineered to flawlessly match her natural complexion. Her pouty lips were filled with fat sucked out of her stomach and ass. Even her long, lustrous hair was full of extensions and expensive hair products. She was every bit as obsessed with beauty as Dr. Mahendru. They were mirror images of each other.

Star knew her mother was repulsed by her obesity. Star could see the disgust on her mother's face every time she looked at her and in every sarcastic word she uttered about her appearance. Her so-called "words of encouragement" were just mean-spirited jabs that hurt and sent Star scurrying to the candy store in defiance. She hadn't taken her daughter to a movie premiere or a public event in years, not since the baby fat had multiplied.

Without consulting a doctor or a health specialist of any sort, her mother diagnosed Star with Prader-Willi Syndrome at the age of four, mistaking a normal healthy appetite for a condition characterized by an inability to efficiently convert fat into energy, leading to intense hunger pangs and a constant, insatiable urge to eat. Her solution was to starve her young daughter, putting locks on the refrigerator and pantry and restricting her to 750 calories a day. Star rebelled, hoarding food in her room and binging on junk food at school. Each time she was caught with candy and pastries stuffed under her mattress, in her mother's mind it reconfirmed her diagnosis. Her daughter was sick. She couldn't stop eating. Her hideous corpulence was ample evidence.

Now, as Star's body consumed itself and she shed pounds by the hour, gnawing hunger pains turning her guts inside out, her cries for food seemed to her anorexic mother like another symptom of her disease.

"Mom, please! I'm dying! I'm so hungry!"

"You're not dying. You're becoming beautiful! The treatment is working! Look at you! You're almost skinny!"

Star turned and looked at herself in one of the full-length mirrors her mother had hung on the back of every door in the house as a punishment, to remind her of what a fat cow she had allowed herself to become. Only now, the girl who looked back at her was not fat at all. There were still a few bulges here and there. Her hips were still wide and her thighs were thicker than they should have been, but far from the elephantine pillars they had been just yesterday. The rolls of fat under her chin had reduced from two to one. Her FUPA (fat upper-pussy area) as her mother called it, a large roll of gelatinous flesh that bulged out from just below her navel and hung down over vagina, had completely disappeared. She was losing weight, a dramatic, terrifying amount of weight in so short a time. She must have dropped seventy pounds in the thirty-six hours since she'd had the treatment.

"Something's wrong, Mom. I'm losing too much weight."

Her mother waved her off with a flick of the wrist, a chuckle, and an exasperated roll of her eyes.

"Don't be silly, Star. You can never lose too much weight. As Wallis Simpson, the Duchess of Windsor, said, 'A woman can't be too skinny or too rich.' If you're hungry, here's a rice cake." She pulled out a pack of rice cakes she'd stashed in her oversized Prada handbag and reached inside to grab one of the crisp, Styrofoam-textured discs from the package.

Snarling, Star launched herself across the room, leaping like some sort of overweight housecat attacking a bag of catnip, and snatched the entire package from her mother's hands. She crashed against the kitchen wall in a heap, knocking over the table in the kitchen nook, denting the drywall, and smashing one of the kitchen chairs. She began mindlessly shoveling handfuls of rice cakes into her mouth.

"Jesus! What's gotten into you? That's disgusting! I said you could have one. You give those back, young lady! You're eating like an animal!"

Star watched her mother reach for her food, and a sudden, overwhelming rage surged through her. Her lips peeled away from her teeth, and a snarl rumbled up from her throat. She lashed out so suddenly and savagely, her mother barely had time to react before Star's curiously elongated canines clamped down on her hand.

 **8.** **"S**HE BIT me! I feel terrible. Cramps. I can't move," Alexis groaned.

"Where is she now?"

"I pushed her inside her room and locked it from the outside. She can't get out."

Trevor had a moment to wonder why her daughter's room locked from the outside.

"I can't move!"

"It's from the bite. I think she may have some kind of neurotoxin in her saliva. The effect should pass soon. Has she had anything to eat?"

"No. She keeps trying to get to the food, but I won't let her. She's trying to undo all the work you did!"

"Listen, Mrs. Mourning. Something went wrong with the procedure. You have to feed her, and I mean *a lot*. Do you understand? She needs a lot of food or your daughter will die."

There was a long pause.

"Do you hear me, Mrs. Mourning?"

"I—I can't do that."

"You have to. Your daughter is losing weight too rapidly. She's starving to death. You have to feed her."

"But she'll get fat again. You should see how she looks. She's lost so much weight. She looks gorgeous! The procedure worked, Doctor!"

The flight attendant was heading toward Trevor, staring at the phone in his hand. He had only a few seconds before she would tell him to turn off his phone.

"I'll be there in about four and a half hours. If you don't feed her, she'll be dead by then. She needs to eat every two hours."

"Every two hours! I'm not doing that! You're trying to make my little baby fat again!"

The flight attendant was standing directly above him now. "Sir, you have to turn off your phone. We're getting ready for takeoff."

"I'm a doctor. I have a patient on the phone. It's a critical life-or-death situation. Please, please indulge me for just a few more minutes, okay?"

"I'm sorry, but you have to hang up."

"One minute? Come on, be cool, okay? I'll be off in one minute. A little girl is going to die if I can't make her mother understand what she needs to do."

The desperation in his voice made the flight attendant pause. She looked out into the main coach cabin. Trevor turned to look and saw a steely eyed man wearing a dusty brown leather jacket over a white T-shirt and jeans.

The man undid his seatbelt and started getting out of his seat.

Air marshal. Fuck.

"Please?"

She waved the man off, and he returned to his seat. His hard eyes were still fixed on Trevor.

"You've got one minute," the flight attendant whispered, wagging a finger at him in stern warning.

"Thank you. Thanks so much."

Trevor cupped his hand over the cell phone.

"Mrs. Mourning? Are you still there?"

"I'm here."

"You cannot let your daughter die just because you want her to look beautiful. I know the pressure society puts on women to be thin and beautiful. Hell, I make my living off it, but there's no way she's going to gain any weight right now, no matter how much she eats. What she will do is *die* if she doesn't eat. What do you want, Mrs. Mourning? A live daughter or a thin corpse?"

Another pause. "Okay. I'll feed her."

"Oh, and Mrs. Mourning?"

"Yes?"

"Be very careful. The treatment might make her a bit... unpredictable. Don't let her bite you again."

"Why would she bite me again?"

"Because she's hungry."

**9.** **T**HE FLIGHT was maddening. Trevor's mind was filled with images of carnage. He imagined the legendary actress Alexis Mourning devoured by her only child. He wished he could make the plane go faster. He kept casting glances over at Dr. Ebersol and could see the same stress and impatience etched into his colleagues features, but there was something there besides the worry—seething rage. He was clearly incensed by the situation Trevor had put him—the entire clinic—in. Trevor accepted his role in the debacle, but he wasn't the only person culpable in this. As far as he was concerned, they had all asked for it: the clinic, Alexis Mourning and her daughter, even Lelani Sims.

They had come to him looking for a miracle, unhappy with what nature had given them. They wanted to be skinny at any cost. He had warned them the treatment had only undergone animal testing, that it was an unapproved treatment. He had warned them all there might be unknown side effects. They didn't care. Anything to be skinny. So he had provided them with the miracle they were seeking.

Trevor grew up in Northwest Philadelphia, Germantown, the only child of a single mom, a scared white kid in a predominantly Black neighborhood. Every day of his young life had been affected by the lack of money. Years later he still carried the painful memory of hearing his mother weep in the late hours when she thought he was asleep as she tried to figure out how she was going to pay bills more numerous than her twenty thousand-dollar-a-year paycheck could cover. He remembered her working two jobs, coming home exhausted, sometimes too tired to eat by the time she'd finished cooking dinner for Trevor. Even now, he remembered how he felt going to the store to buy groceries with food stamps after his mother lost one of her jobs, enduring the judgmental stares and words of ridicule from the other kids.

One of Trevor's earliest memories was of walking home from school down Germantown Avenue, passing shops full of food, clothes, records, and toys he could not afford, watching his school-mates ride by on the bus he could not afford to ride and wave at him or make faces. It was a four-mile walk from Henry H. Houston School in Mount Airy to his little home in Germantown. For Trevor, his choice was to ride the bus or eat lunch. His mother could not afford to buy him a bus pass and buy him lunch. So he walked.

He would leave Germantown Avenue and take the side streets, staring in awe at the beautiful roads lined with sugar maples, fifty-foot white pines, lush willow oaks, and hundred-foot sycamores, huge Colonial mini-mansions creeping with ivy, overlooking sprawling green lawns. Brand-new Lincolns, Cadillacs, Mercedes-Benzes, and Volvos sat in the driveways. Inside, warm and cozy with full bellies, were happy kids with moms who didn't cry at night.

When Trevor arrived home each afternoon to the dilapidated three-story row home he shared with his mother, he would make himself a peanut butter and jelly sandwich and sit down to do his homework while he waited for her to come home and cook dinner. On Mondays, Wednesdays, and Fridays, when his mother worked her second job, Trevor would make his own dinner and put himself to sleep. He was ten years old when his mother first began working two jobs. Sometimes his mother would wake him up when she got home and would hug him and they would dream together. They would talk about him going off to college one day, getting a doctorate degree and becoming a famous scientist and living in a big house with lots of food and toys like the kids in Mount Airy and Chestnut Hill. Trevor would promise his mother that he would buy her a big shiny new car and take her traveling all over the world. She told him she was working so hard to make sure he could go to college one day and have everything he dreamed of. Trevor never got to buy his mother that new car. She died of obesity-related diabetes just before he graduated high school. Her only wish had been that he make a success of himself, and Trevor was not going to let her down.

When Trevor was in college, he watched a documentary about the two doctors who invented breast implants. They made millions and became celebrities in the medical world. That was the type of success Trevor wanted. But he knew plastic surgery was a dying science. The future was in genetic engineering. What the public called "gene doping" was poised to make plastic surgery—as well as the entire diet and fitness industry—obsolete. The fact that gene doping was illegal was ridiculous in his mind. He had never met a professional or Olympic-level athlete who wasn't on some form of performance-enhancing drugs. Yet the public celebrated the ones who didn't get caught and ostracized the athletes who tested dirty. *How can there be cheaters when everyone is doing it?*

Like "natural" professional bodybuilders, the "natural athlete" has long been a myth. In every sport, from baseball to basketball, football, boxing, tennis, cycling, track, swimming, mixed martial arts, and even volleyball, performance-enhancing drugs are the norm, not the exception. There has been an arms race going on in sports since the sixties, with every athlete struggling for an edge, and in that arms race, genetic engineering stood poised to become a nuclear bomb.

Sports fans want to see records broken year after year, in every sports season, in every Olympics. How do they think that can happen without some kind of pharmaceutical assistance? But the sports industry has to keep up the illusion. Fuck the illusion! Why not make athletes as fast and powerful as they can be? Why not make women as beautiful as they can be? If science can do it, and the public obviously wants it, why not?

Trevor was building up his own head of indignant, unrepentant anger. He knew he would be made out to be the bad guy, crucified by the media, perhaps even incarcerated and/or sued for millions when this was exposed. Despite their efforts to contain it, this desperate flight back to the states to try to avert what seemed an inevitable fate, the media would catch wind of it. It would be the top story of the year if Alexis Mourning got eaten by her daughter because of a genetic weight-loss treatment.

Trevor thought about the others he'd given the treatment to, those he hadn't contacted yet: the host of a top-rated televised singing contest in LA; an executive chef in Austin; a famous young country singer; a former Republican speaker of the house; an African American talk-show host; a rotund hip-hop artist; two pop-singers who combined were one of the most famous couples on the planet; and at least six others. It was only a matter of time before Dr. Ebersol started asking him about his other patients, and Trevor still had no idea what he was going to do.

"What are we supposed to do when we get there?"

Dr. Ebersol roused from his own deep thoughts. His face seemed to have aged a decade since they boarded the plane. His eyes were vacant, looking through Trevor at some horror from his darkest imagination. Trevor knew exactly what the man had been so intensely contemplating. He was trying to imagine how profound someone's hunger would have to be to make them eat another human being in the middle of a city with supermarkets and restaurants fifteen or twenty minutes away.

"What?"

Dr. Ebersol's eyes focused on Trevor as if he was just now aware of the man's presence beside him. He regarded Trevor with obvious disdain. A sneer of disgust twisted his features.

"I was just wondering what exactly we're going to do when we get back to the states. I don't exactly have an antidote. What are we supposed to do here? How are we going to help them?"

That faraway look returned to Ebersol's eyes. He looked like he was going into shock.

"David?"

His eyes focused again. This time he looked less angry. He just looked defeated. "We need to get them back to the clinic or to a hospital, and then you need to figure out how to extract that DNA from their cells."

Trevor shook his head. "That's not possible. Once something is part of your genetic makeup, it can't just be taken out."

Dr. Ebersol jabbed him in the chest with his finger. "If you put it in there, you can take it out, or put something else in to counteract it. Make another retrovirus, one that will curb their appetite and help them gain weight."

He punctuated each word with another jab. Trevor rubbed his chest and pouted.

"You want me to just pull that out of my ass? It's not that simple. You know how long something like that would take? Isolating and extracting the right DNA strand, synthesizing the virus, the clinical trials? Look, I've been thinking. Maybe we're going about this the wrong way. Maybe we should just let this thing run its course."

"What are you talking about? What do you mean, 'Let it run its course'?"

Trevor lowered his voice to a whisper and cupped a hand over his mouth so the passengers around them wouldn't overhear what he was saying. "Let's say Alexis doesn't feed her daughter, and the same thing happens to her that happened to Lelani Simms's fiancé. It seems to me that wouldn't be such a bad thing. It might just solve all of our problems. She kills her mother, that's one witness gone, and then she starves to death herself, both witnesses gone. No one is going to trace this back to us."

Dr. Ebersol was practically turning colors in his effort to restrain his rage and keep his voice at a whisper. "And what about Lelani?"

"If she's starving like you say she is, she'll probably be dead before we even get there."

"And what happens, you fucking amoral imbecile, if they just keep feeding? What happens if Lelani starts making her way through the entire building? What happens if—after killing her mom—Star kills the maid, the gardener, the fucking pool boy? And what about all the others you've given this shit to? Have you contacted them yet?"

Trevor slowly shook his head.

"I didn't think so. What if they start going on a rampage and eating everyone around them?"

"I think we can contain it. They'd probably just raid their own pantries first and then hit the nearest restaurant. I don't know why Lelani didn't just order takeout or drive herself to a buffet or something. I don't think what she did can be considered a normal reaction to hunger, even intense hunger. There are people starving to death in Africa who aren't eating each other. I say we just monitor them."

Dr. Ebersol shook his head. "Monitor them? More than a dozen people? And how do you propose we do that?"

"We hire private detectives. We pay them to keep their mouths shut and report anything suspicious."

"And what do we tell them to do when they see the person they're supposed to be watching chowing down on their neighbor?" Ebersol asked.

Trevor shrugged. "I don't know. Tranquilize them. Subdue them. Bring them back to the clinic. I really don't think that's going to happen though."

"And what do we do with them when we get them back to the clinic?"

"I guess I'd try to cure them."

"So why the fuck wouldn't we start there? Why wait until they've lost their fucking minds and eaten half the neighborhood before we try to cure them?" Ebersol asked.

"Because I don't know if I can, and if I can't, what do we do with them? We can't have a baker's dozen of the world's rich and famous drop dead at a medical resort in Cancun. You don't think that'll look suspicious? They'd be better off dying in their beds or getting shot by the police. It would be cleaner that way."

"Getting shot by police trying to eat someone's kid or something is cleaner?"

Trevor shrugged again. "At least we wouldn't be involved."

Ebersol grabbed Trevor by his lapels and shook him. "But we *are* involved, you fucking asshole! And you think it wouldn't get traced back to us?"

Trevor jerked away from Ebersol and nervously looked around the cabin. "Shhh! Keep your voice down. We still don't even know if everyone is going to react the way Lelani did. That was one isolated incident. All we know is that Star Mourning is really hungry. We don't know for a fact that she's going to start eating people. We could be blowing all of this out of proportion. Models are fucking crazy anyway. I'm sure Lelani had a lot of problems before I treated her. Maybe the cannibalism thing was an accident."

"An accident? How do you figure that?"

"Maybe she was just being opportunistic. She got into a fight with her fiancé, things got physical, and Lelani killed him by accident. Then she ate him because he was there, and she was hungry, and he was already dead."

Trevor could see Dr. Ebersol considering it. It was obvious this scenario hadn't entered his mind before and he wanted to believe it. Trevor wanted to believe it too.

"Maybe all we have to do is meet with my other clients and tell them they are going to have to eat a lot more than normal, and that's the end of it. Maybe prescribe some type of high-calorie protein shake or something to eat between meals?"

"I suppose. We'll see soon if Lelani was just an isolated incident."

Below them, water gave way to land. San Diego, California, came into view, a vast expanse of lights. They would be landing in LA soon. Trevor would be taking a car to the home of Alexis Mourning, and Dr. Ebersol would be continuing on to Austin, Texas.

Neither had a clue how bad the day would end. They had no idea what they were getting into. Not the slightest idea.

**10.**

"I BROUGHT YOU some food, dear. Oh my God!"

The tray of cold cuts, crackers, and pâté spilled from Alexis Mourning's hands, and a scream tore from her throat. Her daughter was sitting on the edge of the bed, cannibalizing her own hand. Her three middle fingers had been completely removed. The naked phalanges stuck out of Star's mouth as she gnawed at them, probing them for the last morsels of flesh before moving on to her thumb.

"Stop!" Alexis shouted.

Star let out a wounded cry and then scampered over to the pile of spilled food smeared onto the polished mahogany floor. Star scooped up the pâté and shoved the entire quarter-pound slice into her mouth, chewing quickly and swallowing. She grabbed a fistful of crackers in one hand, cold cuts in the hand she'd almost chewed off, sat on the floor—clearly oblivious to her mother's presence—and devoured all of it. She continued to moan like a wounded dog while shoveling food into her mouth. A torrent of tears streamed from her crimson-rimmed eyes.

"What's wrong, Star? You're scaring me."

"I'm so hungry. I feel like I'm dying. I need more food," her daughter cried between bites.

Alexis remembered what the doctor told her about giving her daughter as much to eat as she wanted, but everything she'd ever learned about being a woman rebelled against the idea of letting her daughter glut herself.

"That—that's not enough food? You don't want to get fat again, do you?"

It was a ridiculous question. In the last four hours, Star Mourning had lost another twenty pounds. She now had the body her mother had always dreamt of. The jiggle was gone from her belly. It was now totally flat and even a bit concave. Her hips were almost completely gone; just enough remained now to give her a slight curve and emphasize the slenderness of her waist. The dimpled cellulose that had been clustered around her ass and thighs had melted away, leaving stretch-marked skin that hung loosely from her atrophied muscles. A few weeks in the gym was all her daughter would need to tighten up those muscles, and any of the skilled surgeons at the Aphrodite Clinic could easily correct the loose skin and stretch marks, Alexis thought. She smiled appreciatively at her daughter, admiring her increasingly emaciated appearance, heedless of the gleam of insanity sparkling in the young girl's eyes, and forgetting the fact that she'd walked in on the child feasting on her own fingers. All that mattered to Alexis was that her daughter was finally skinny.

"I'm starving!"

Star scrambled to her feet and rushed past her mother, heading for the kitchen and the locked refrigerator. She leapt up onto a chair in the parlor and snatched the heavy drapes down from the window. She pulled the curtain rod free from the thick satin drapes while still running toward the kitchen in full sprint. Gripping the thick, wrought-iron curtain rod in both hands, Star took a swing at the lock on the refrigerator, gouging the stainless steel. She swung several more times before the lock finally gave way.

Her mother entered the kitchen behind her just as Star opened the refrigerator and began pulling food off the shelves and scarfing it down. Alexis stood a safe distance away, terrified for the first time that her daughter might be losing her mind. She pulled out her cell phone and tried once more to phone the doctor.

Dr. Trevor Adams didn't answer his phone. *He must still be on the plane,* she thought. In desperation, Alexis phoned her psychiatrist.

"Dr. Linder? This is Alexis. I need your help." Her voice choked and she let out a strangled sob.

"What is it? What's happened?"

Alexis cleared her throat and wiped away an unexpected sprinkle of tears.

"I think my daughter's going crazy."

"Star? What's wrong with her? Is it her weight again?"

"Yes. I mean, no. Kind of. She keeps eating. She lost a bunch of weight since we came back from the clinic, but she's eating everything in sight! She bit me and then she ate her own fingers when I wouldn't give her any food."

"She—did you say she ate her own fingers?"

Alexis sobbed again. She covered her mouth with her hand and wept.

"Oh, God. Oh, God!"

"Alexis? Alexis? Are you all right? Did you say your daughter ate her own fingers?"

"Yes! She ate them down to the bone! Three of them! She's raiding the refrigerator right now! What's wrong with her?"

"I-I don't know. Maybe it's some extreme type of binge-eating disorder coupled with dermatophagia. Has she ever eaten her own skin before to your knowledge?"

"No. I'd never allow such a horrible thing. What's dermatophagia?"

"The eating of one's own skin. It can be symptoms of a number of different things, but rarely is it caused by hunger. Stress is a major cause. Many victims feel stress and picking and eating their own skin is a form of self-soothing. Self-image issues are another of the main causes. They may pick their skin in the hopes of correcting some perceived irregularity in their complexion, though they invariably end up making themselves look worse. Skin-picking may also provide needed stimulation for the nervous system when someone is bored or under-stimulated."

"You didn't hear me. She didn't just chew on her skin. She ate her own damn fingers and she did it because she was hungry! What the hell is wrong with her?"

There was a pause. She heard the doctor clear his throat.

"Self-cannibalism, autosarcophagy, is pretty rare. I've never encountered a true case of it myself, though I have read about it. A Chilian artist named Marco Evaristti held a dinner party for a few of his close friends back in 1996 and served a pasta dish with meatballs made from beef and his own belly fat extracted during a liposuction treatment. He claimed he did it as an artistic statement. That may or may not have been the symptom of a mental disorder. That same year, a deathrow inmate in Texas pulled out his eye and ate it. There was a pretty famous case of vorarephilia when a German man, Bernd Jürgen Brande, cut off and ate his own cooked penis before being killed and eaten by Armin Meiwes, the 'Rotenburg Cannibal', who also ate some of Brande's cooked penis.."

Alexis gasped.

"That's disgusting! Why the hell are you telling me all this? I need you to come over and take care of my little girl."

"If she's hurting herself, the best place for her is probably a hospital or a mental facility. Now, I can suggest a few places—"

"A nuthouse! You want me to put my little girl in an insane asylum?" Alexis asked with an exaggerated, theatrical tone of outrage.

"Not an asylum. A place where she can rest and be looked after where she won't be able to hurt herself."

"I—I don't know. Do you really think that's the right thing to do?"

"I think it's what's best for her."

**EDNESDAY, 9:35 A.M.**
Brian was hungry. He was already on his way to the restaurant, and there was plenty of food there, but he almost felt like he wouldn't make it. In addition to his growling stomach and his rapidly shrinking waistline, he felt a deep existential dread. He literally felt like he would be dead within minutes if he didn't eat something right now.

Brian had never wanted the treatment in the first place. It had been a birthday present from his wife. Going to the gym, taking up kickboxing, and running had all been working, but she had wanted to surprise him with something guaranteed to get the job done faster. He'd been ambiguous about the idea from the start.

"The doctors at the clinic say it's a permanent weight-loss solution. One treatment and you're guaranteed to drop as much as fifty pounds a day! That's amazing, isn't it?"

"Sounds dangerous. Has it been tested? Are you sure it's approved?"

She shook her head.

"It isn't approved in America yet. It's a brand-new treatment, but this is one of the most famous and exclusive cosmetic surgery and weight-loss clinics in the world. They have all the best doctors, and they use the latest medical procedures. Their clients are billionaires, movie stars, and rock stars."

"Sounds expensive. How much does it cost?" he asked, and then braced himself for the answer. His worst fears of financial extravagance fell short of the reality.

"It was fifty thousand dollars."

"Fifty thousand! You spent fifty thousand of my money on this?"

"Our money. We're married, remember? What's yours is mine. And I did it for you. This way, you won't have to spend so much time at the gym, and you can spend more time with me!"

She'd been ecstatic. Brian sucked down his anger as much as he could. He made a pretty good living, well into the six figures, but he was not exactly wealthy. Fifty thousand was more than half their savings and it had taken him six years to save up that much. Now that he was married, it would probably take twice that long to build it back up.

He closed his eyes and took several deep breaths before speaking. He knew he had to phrase his words carefully. "But I like going to the gym, and I was saving that money for a house."

"We still have enough for a house. You only need to put down 20 percent. Houses aren't that expensive, unless you were planning on buying a mansion. I bought it for you. You're going. That's it. I already paid for the plane tickets and everything anyway. We can turn it into a mini-vacation. You'll be happy we did this. You'll see."

She'd been right. He was happy. They had a blast in Cancun, lounging on the beach and drinking the most powerful margaritas on the planet, deep-sea fishing, visiting Mayan ruins, swimming with the dolphins. Even the treatment hadn't been bad. It was just one little intramuscular injection.

"That's it?" Brian asked the doctor, still holding the cotton swab to the injection site on his thigh.

The young doctor, who looked like he'd just graduated from college, smiled and nodded. "Yup. That's it. You need to spend the night here just to make sure it took. If not, we'll try again in the morning."

"How will you know if it took?" Brian asked.

"We'll weigh you in the morning. On average, someone your size can fluctuate between five and seven pounds between the evening after eating all day and after sleeping for eight hours. We'll be looking for something more dramatic than that. At least a twenty-pound loss."

"Twenty-pounds? In one night?" Brian scoffed.

"At least."

Dr. Trevor Adams held Brian's gaze without the slightest hint of humor. He affected an air of supreme self-assurance.

Brian instantly disliked the man. *Cocky little prick.*

The next morning, Brian woke thirty pounds lighter and ravenously hungry.

"The hunger is normal. Your metabolism is on hyper-drive. Take advantage of it. Eat whatever you like. We have the best chefs on the island here at the clinic. You don't have to worry about watching what you eat ever again."

By the time Brian left the island, he was a hundred pounds lighter. He had to admit, he looked great, but the hunger just seemed to get worse the more weight he lost. He wondered what would happen when there was no more fat left for his body to consume. There was no way someone could continue to burn a hundred thousand calories a day. You would have to eat nonstop to feed such a metabolism. As a chef, he knew the highest-calorie foods. They were some of his favorites. But even if he ate every fried, sugary, buttery food he could think of, dripping in gravy with a creamy dessert to follow, he'd never be able to eat that many calories.

The restaurant was only five miles away on Third Street. In normal traffic, he would have been there in ten minutes. But rush-hour traffic had slowed to a crawl.

"Fuck! Come on! Move!"

The fire in his belly had increased. Brian felt like he could feel his body eating itself, turning fat and muscle into adenosine triphosphate and incinerating it. The pants he was wearing had just been purchased yesterday when he realized his entire wardrobe no longer fit. In fewer than twenty-four hours, he'd gone down two more sizes, and his new pants were now sagging off him. He was wasting away.

He was almost to the Oltorf exit, just two exits away from Third Street, but he didn't think he could make it. There was an Indian/Texas fusion restaurant on Oltorf he'd always wanted to try. He jerked the wheel to the right onto the shoulder and headed toward the nearest exit. He never saw the police cruiser racing down the shoulder, never even felt the impact.

Brian's neck snapped cleanly when his head smacked the dashboard, and he was simply gone.

12.

WEDNESDAY,
9:37 A.M.
Officer Angel
Velasquez blinked several times, trying to clear the fog from his head. He wiped what he thought was sweat from his eyes and his hand came away red. He was bleeding, a head wound. Blood poured down his face from a gash that looked like his forehead had grown a vagina and it was that time of the month. Instead of fear, he felt anger. "That sonovabitch pulled out right in front of me!"

He opened the car door and staggered out of his vehicle, almost stepping out into traffic. It wouldn't have mattered; traffic was at a standstill. The police cruiser was smashed. The bumper was completely crushed, and the hood had folded up like an accordion. The big, black Yukon that had crashed into him didn't look too bad except for the bumper, which was hanging off, and the huge dent in the hatch. The guy behind the wheel, however, wasn't moving.

Angel rolled his eyes. *Oh, great. He's probably going to try to sue me. And because I rear-ended him, he'll probably win. Fuck my life.*

But as he got closer and noticed the man's bleeding head tilted at an odd angle, he was pretty sure the guy was dead.

Damn.

He flagged down the ambulance that was racing up behind him. It was en route to the same accident Angel had been en route toward before he'd struck the Kamikaze commuter, but Officer Velasquez suspected this was more urgent than some obese housewife faking whiplash for insurance money.

The ambulance stopped in back of his cruiser, and two EMTs jumped out. One was a huge black guy who looked like he should have been chasing a quarterback across a football field, and the other was a mousy little white woman with brown hair who had all the markings of a meth addict, right down to the rotting teeth and acne scars.

"The driver looks like he needs help. He don't look so good. I think he might be dead. His head might have hit the steering wheel or something."

"Are you okay? Your head's bleeding. Why don't you go back to the ambulance and sit down, okay?" the mousy little meth addict said. Her breath was rancid, like she'd been on a strict diet of Twinkies and road kill.

"No, I'm okay. You just take care of that guy up there." Angel leaned against the cruiser while the EMTs jogged over to the vehicle and went to work. It was hot as hell out, at least one hundred degrees with 60 percent humidity. Too fucking hot to be screwing around in traffic.

The EMTs were fast and efficient. They already had the guy out of the Yukon and onto the gurney and were frantically administering CPR as they raced him back to the ambulance.

"Is he gonna make it?" Angel asked as they passed him.

The big linebacker of an ambulance driver looked at him and shook his head. "At least he was an organ donor," he said, handing Angel the guy's wallet.

Angel flipped it open.

Brian Wubbenna, Austin, Texas, age thirty-seven. In the bottom corner was a little red heart designating him as an organ donor. *Damn. Thirty-seven was too damn young to die. What the fuck was this guy thinking pulling out in front of me like that? At least his organs will do some good. Maybe save some other poor bastard's life.*

13.

WEDNESDAY, 9:52 A.M.

"We've got a donor! There was an accident on I-35 this morning. The guy died instantly. His heart is in excellent condition. They're rushing it over to us now. We need to get you prepped for immediate surgery."

Anthony Berkley had been born with a congenital heart valve defect. He had his first heart attack in the middle of a college basketball game while charging up the court for a lay-up. Since then, he'd had two more and was informed he'd be dead in a year unless he received a transplant. He was only twenty-two, six foot eight, 265 pounds, good-looking, clean-cut, had his entire life ahead of him, but his failing heart made him doubt if that life would account for more than twenty-four years. He was on the top of the donors' list, but that didn't mean a damn thing if they couldn't find him a heart, and it had begun to look like that would never happen. Anthony had already given up hope when the doctor came in with the good news.

"Who was he? The donor, I mean?"

"He was thirty-seven years old and in good physical condition. Not an ounce of excess body fat on this guy from what they tell me. You lucked out."

WEDNESDAY, 10:31 A.M.

Nurses surrounded Anthony, shaving his chest and washing it with a special antiseptic cleaning solution. The anesthesiologist attached heart and blood pressure monitors to his arms, head, and ribs and then began an IV fentanyl drip.

"Okay, I need you to count backwards from fifty," the doctor said.

"Fifty, forty-nine, forty-eight, forty-seven…"

He started counting but was unconscious before he could get to forty-six.

WEDNESDAY, 5:40 P.M.

Anthony woke from surgery in recovery, and for the first time in months he didn't feel out of breath. He was woozy from the drugs and his throat felt dry and scratchy from the air tube they'd shoved down his throat during the procedure, but other than that, he felt pretty damn good.

"How are you feeling?"

"Pretty good. My throat hurts. Did everything go okay?"

The doctor nodded. "It went perfectly. The sore throat is normal. The nurse will bring you something to drink."

"No ice cream? I thought you were supposed to get ice cream after surgery."

"If you like," the doctor answered, still studying Anthony's chart, checking the EKG.

"I think I do. I'm hungry as hell for some reason."

"That's normal after surgery. You've essentially been fasting for twenty-four hours."

Anthony put his hand over the sutures in his chest. "It feels funny. Like it's about to beat right out of my chest."

The doctor nodded. "That's normal too. Because the nerves leading to the heart are cut during the operation, your new heart beats faster than a normal heart, about a hundred to a hundred and ten beats per minute compared to about seventy beats per minute for a normal healthy heart."

Anthony rubbed the bandages around his chest and took a deep breath. There was a hint of panic in his eyes. "It feels like thunder."

"You'll get used to it."

><

SATURDAY, 6:06 A.M.

The hunger woke Anthony from a sound sleep. His belly was on fire. His appetite had steadily increased since the surgery. The room was dark and deathly quiet except for the blinking lights and the whir and hum of the monitoring equipment. He groped for the nurse's call button and rang it.

The night nurse hadn't left for the day yet. She walked into the room followed by the day nurse. She did a reasonably good job of masking her annoyance.

"Yes?"

"I'm starving! I need something to eat."

"We'll be serving breakfast in a few hours. You just hold tight."

"No! I need to eat now!"

Over the past three days, he'd had countless X-rays and blood tests and been pumped full of anti-rejection medications. Through it all, he could think of nothing but the next meal. Last night, his mother brought him a grilled chicken sandwich from some healthy restaurant downtown and some baked fries. He'd scarfed it down and then begged her for a couple of cheeseburgers.

"The doctor said you have to keep your weight down or you might put too much strain on your new heart," his mother said.

"Do I look like I'm gaining weight?" Anthony asked.

His mother, a young thirty-eight-year-old who'd given birth to Anthony at the tender age of sixteen, shook her head. Anthony appeared withered and shrunken, even more sickly than he had before receiving the new heart. It was understandable after such an arduous surgery, but he seemed to be getting worse, not better. He was concerned that his body may be rejecting the new heart.

The bones in Anthony's face were prominent. It looked like a skull with skin pulled tight around it. Like the face of a mummy. His ribcage protruded through his skin. Before he'd been admitted to the hospital, before the life-saving surgery, he'd been muscular and robust. He had looked very much like the NBA player he'd once dreamt of becoming. Now he was an emaciated shadow of his former self.

His mother smiled, trying hard to keep up the appearance of optimism, but Anthony could see the concern on her face. He knew he looked like shit.

"You're right. I'm sorry. Whatever you like."

She'd brought him three cheeseburgers, fries, and a milkshake. He scarfed down the food without tasting it and then fell asleep. The fire in his belly had been temporarily assuaged.

Now he was awake again, and his mother was nowhere to be found. His appetite had increased exponentially since his last meal. It felt like he hadn't eaten for weeks.

Anthony pulled the IV tube from his wrist and pulled off the EKG lead wires. He swung his legs over the side of the bed and began to stand. "Something's wrong. I'm starving! I need food!"

The nurse was young and pretty, though several pounds overweight. Not obese, but pleasantly plump. She had a wide flat ass, huge hips, and large breasts supported by a belly that was only slightly smaller. She wasn't the type of girl a guy like him would ever call girlfriend, at least not publicly. She was the type of girl you banged on the side because she was more sexually adventurous than your real girlfriend, your showpiece. She was what his friends called a "Moped"—fun to ride, but you wouldn't want anyone to see you with it.

She panicked as Anthony pushed his way past her. His elbow brushed against her chest, and Anthony was surprised to find his appetite respond to the contact. He began salivating. He looked at her, drooling.

She backed up, covering her mouth, looking horrified. "Sir! You need to stay calm. You need to keep your IV in."

He was surprised by how strong he felt. Despite his nagging hunger, he didn't feel weak or dizzy, the way he usually felt when he hadn't eaten. But he had eaten and eaten well. He must have consumed more than ten thousand calories yesterday.

What the fuck is wrong with me? he wondered.

Something was definitely wrong with his mouth. His teeth felt all wrong. Longer. Sharper. He dragged his tongue over his canines and tasted his own blood as the sharp points sliced through his taste buds. Something wasn't right. He wondered if they'd given him a heart from a werewolf or something. Maybe they'd used him in some sort of experiment?

THE nurse ran to the door and called for an orderly while Anthony shambled past her, heading for where? He wasn't sure. The cafeteria maybe? All he knew was there was food somewhere in the hospital, and he needed to find it before he died of starvation.

Something's not right. I just ate. Why am I so hungry?

He approached the nurses' station and could smell potato chips and candy. No wonder all the nurses in this hospital were overweight. He walked behind the counter and pushed the middle-aged Latina manning the station aside as she tried to prevent him from entering.

"You're not allowed back here. Oof!"

Anthony shoved her to the floor and wrenched open a desk drawer. Inside was a half-eaten bag of barbecue potato chips and several candy bars and meal replacement bars along with a bag of sunflower seeds. He opened the packages one by one and shoved the bars into his mouth whole, chewing and swallowing rapidly. He turned up the bag of sunflower seeds and poured its contents into his mouth, eating them, shells and all.

"Okay, son. Time to go back to your room."

The orderly was wide and doughy, like the nurses. He was shorter than Anthony by at least five inches and looked like he hadn't seen a gym in years. Another orderly approached. This guy was under six feet, Latino, with tattoos peeking out from beneath his hospital scrubs. He had a shaved head, muscular arms, and looked like he was probably a bad-ass when he wasn't changing bedpans. He was the one who made the mistake of grabbing Anthony.

Some instinct took over, something dark and primal, feral, that had been hiding deep inside Anthony. Deep in his genetic memory, from his Neanderthal, evolutionary past. He bared his teeth, and before the man could react, Anthony lunged for his throat and sank his teeth into the man's trachea. He bit down, crushing the orderly's windpipe. A whistling sound, like a broken flute, whined from the bleeding hole where Anthony's iron-tipped fangs had pierced his voice box. With a jerk of his head, Anthony tore out the man's throat. The muscular orderly with the gangland tattoos fell to the hospital floor, painting everyone red with the arterial spray spurting from his brutally savaged throat. He clamped both hands around his neck in an attempt to stop the flow of blood.

"Oh, my God! What the hell did you do to him? Call security!" the nurse yelled, and the other orderly leapt into action.

He shoved Anthony backward, away from his fallen partner, and snatched up a phone.

"I need security up here right away! A patient just attacked one of the staff!"

The nurse knelt down, began applying pressure to the wound, and ordered the orderly to get her some towels and bandages.

Anthony stood above them, slowly chewing the large hunk of flesh he'd torn from the man's throat. It felt good going down. He could feel it soothing his hunger pains, but only slightly. He needed more.

More nurses and a couple of doctors arrived. They lifted the orderly onto a gurney and whisked him away down the hall before Anthony could take another bite out of him. Security arrived too. They surrounded him with their hands on their guns. There were two uniformed police officers in addition to five armed security guards.

"Get on the ground! Now!" barked one of the cops, a balding, middle-aged man with an athletic build and a nervous, twitchy manner. He seemed ill-suited to the job. He had more of a professorial air about him than one of law enforcement. He held a taser in one hand and pepper spray in the other.

Anthony bared his blood-drenched fangs, and the officers recoiled. He saw a potential meal in every one of them. The orderly's flesh had tasted wonderful. It had briefly taken the edge off his mind-numbing, soul-consuming hunger. He looked from one officer to the next, spotting a blonde woman with an oddly shaped mouth that appeared to have been altered somehow, like she'd had cosmetic surgery to repair a cleft lip. She had the wide hips and ass that seemed to be common to this little corner of Austin.

Anthony began to drool as he took in her curves, imagining how the bloody meat would taste, no longer thinking it odd to consider such things. He had completely abdicated all reason to his appetite. His animal brain had taken control, and it knew how to feed the hunger far better than Anthony did. It knew what it needed. Meat.

"Jesus!" the woman said, staring at his gore-streaked fangs and taking a step backward as Anthony locked eyes with her and took several steps toward her. She aimed her pepper spray at him, preparing to douse him with it.

"I'm hungry! I'm so hungry!" Anthony moaned.

"I said get down!" the balding cop shouted, but Anthony took no notice of him. The officer's voice came from somewhere beyond Anthony's hunger, an echo from another plane of existence, another dimension.

"Just calm down, big guy. Let's talk about this. Nobody else has to get hurt here," the blonde cop with the hair-lip said. But she was wrong.

Anthony covered the distance between them in one stride, like he was leaping across a basketball court for a lay-up. He tackled her and bit into her throat, and every muscle in his body locked and vibrated, waves of agony coursing through him as the balding cop hit him with a hundred thousand volts from the taser gun.

Seconds later, Anthony's brand new heart stopped forever.

**14.** IN THE same hospital where Anthony Berkeley was tasered to death by cops while attempting to cannibalize an orderly, Tammy Galindo saw her mother's face for the first time since she'd lost her eyesight four years ago. She had received a cornea transplant, and although the image was blurry, she could see the corners of her mommy's lips pulled back into an unmistakable smile.

It had only been a few days since the surgery, but every day her vision improved by leaps and bounds. Today she was going home with her parents.

Dr. Alonzo Savaresse stood smiling above her. She could make out his perfect white teeth, chiseled bone structure, square jaw, professionally quaffed raven-black hair, and unfortunately crossed eyes.

She smiled back at him as he gave her instructions on how to care for her new eyes. Tammy was hungry again, and she was finding it hard to concentrate on what he was saying.

"Recovery could take anywhere from one to three weeks. If your recovery thus far is any indication, I think you'll be closer to one week than three. Still, there are precautions you need to take while your eyes are healing. You need to try not to rub your eyes. That could detach your retinas and ruin all my good work."

He reached out and ruffled her curly red hair. Tammy smiled wider and giggled a little. She looked like a redheaded Shirley

Temple. Her long curly hair, dimpled cheeks, and brilliant smile had helped compensate for her cloudy white corneas.

"Okay. I won't."

"Good. That's good. Unfortunately, you can't go swimming or play any sports or even go to the playground and hang from the monkey bars or anything for at least two weeks. We don't want you doing anything that will increase blood pressure to the head or the eye. No activity that requires heavy lifting, bending the head lower than the waist, or any straining that requires holding your breath. No riding your bike for a while either. And you should wear sunglasses when you go outside. Your eyes are going to be sensitive to light for a few days. And wear your eye patch at night until you're fully healed. Okay?"

"Yes, sir."

"And Mom, you need to make sure little Tammy here takes her medication exactly as prescribed, and I want to see you both back here in one week," the doctor said, ruffling Tammy's hair once again and giving her dimpled cheeks a pinch for good measure.

Both Tammy and her mother agreed. They left the hospital holding hands while one of the nurses pushed Tammy out to their waiting car in a wheelchair.

"Mom?"

"Yes, baby?"

"Can we stop by McDonald's? I'm starving!"

"What's going on with your little appetite? You just had ice cream and a cookie before we left the hospital."

Tammy shrugged. "They only gave me a little bit. I'm so hungry, Mom. Pleeeeease?"

"Okay. Okay."

D R. TREVOR Adams arrived at the opulent home of actress Alexis Mourning just in time to see the woman's daughter attack two men in a lab coat. They were leading her out of the house when she suddenly turned and slashed one across the face with fingernails that appeared unusually long and thick. The man howled in pain and fell to his knees. The other man was still holding on to the girl's arm when she bit his shoulder. The man punched at her, yelling and shouting, while she tore a large chunk from his deltoid muscle and then climbed up onto his chest and rode him to the ground, biting at his face, neck, and chest, tearing savagely at him with her teeth and claws. Yes, those were definitely claws.

What the fuck did I do? Trevor thought, and then his mercenary nature took over and he wondered if there might be military applications for this little fuck-up. Maybe there was a way to turn this to his advantage and make even bigger profits off it.

In the doorway of the enormous mansion, Alexis Mourning cowered, watching her only daughter brutally destroy the man in the lab coat. Trevor stayed in the car until it was over.

The man whose face Star had slashed ran into the house holding his face together with his hands. Blood poured from between the man's fingertips. The lacerated skin on his cheek hung like cheese cloth from the exposed bone. Trevor could see the man's teeth and gums through the hole in the side of his face.

Alexis went back into the house as well, leaving her daughter alone with the man she was cannibalizing. Trevor watched in horrified fascination as Star Mourning vigorously eviscerated the man, frantically digging at his stomach with her massive claws. Trevor covered his ears to muffle the sound of his agonized cries.

"HELP! Oh, God! Heeeeelp! Aaaaaah! OH, GOD!"

She pulled out the man's intestines and crammed them into her mouth as he shrieked and tried in vain to fend her off. She had both hands deep in his stomach, yanking out organs and eating them whole. The man stopped screaming and was lying on the porch, quivering and convulsing, while Star continued plundering his body for food. Blood poured off the edge of the porch in sheets like a dark red waterfall.

When she was sated, Star Mourning staggered to her feet and walked across the porch. She banged on the door for her mother to let her in. When there was no response, she curled up by the door in a fetal position and fell asleep.

Trevor got out of his car. He didn't know what he could do or say, but he had to do something. What he needed was a tranquilizer. Something to sedate the girl with before she got hungry again. Unfortunately, he hadn't thought that far ahead. Despite what Ebersol told him about Lelani Simms eating her fiancée, he hadn't really expected to find anything like this. He was completely unprepared. Only now did he start thinking seriously about his other patients.

Oh, fuck. This could be happening to all of them. Trevor pulled out his cell phone. It was time to tell Sarai what was going on and pray to God she didn't fire him for this. But first he needed to warn Dr. Ebersol.

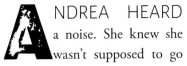NDREA HEARD a noise. She knew she wasn't supposed to go into Mommy and Daddy's room, but she was scared. It sounded like there was a monster in the house.

Something growled. It came from the end of the hall. Mommy and Daddy's room was down there.

Andrea grabbed her Lalaloopsy doll and crawled out of bed. She dragged her blanket and pillow with her as she crept out of the room and tiptoed down the hall where the ferocious noises got louder. It was coming from her parents' room. She stopped in the hallway. Last time Andrea heard noises coming from their room and she'd gone to investigate, she'd seen her daddy on top of her mommy and he'd gotten very angry at her. He told her never to come in their room in the middle of the night again, but she was scared. The noises sounded different this time. Scarier.

"Mommy?"

The growling sounds paused. She heard a snuffling sound, like a dog sniffing. Then someone moaned. It sounded like her mommy.

"Mommy?"

Andrea crept closer to the door. The snuffling sound stopped, replaced by wet smacking sounds like someone eating something wet and juicy. Then there were wet ripping sounds and more moans. Andrea peered through her parents' open door.

Her mommy was on the bed, and there was someone on top of her, but it wasn't Daddy. Daddy was lying on the floor, and his head was gone. Blood pumped from the ragged stump where his head had been. She knew it was Daddy because of his pajamas—soft and blue with pictures of cars on them. Mommy bought him those pajamas for Christmas. She put Andrea's name on the card and said it was from both of them. Now they were all torn and bloody.

Andrea stared at her mommy, and her mommy stared back. There was a scary woman on top of her with wild wooly hair. The woman wasn't looking at Andrea. She was eating Andrea's mommy. Biting her again and again and ripping at her with big sharp nails. The scary woman had her head buried in her mommy's stomach, and she was chewing and pulling stuff out of her.

Her mommy's lips were moving, like she was trying to speak, but her mouth was filled with blood that bubbled out and ran across her cheeks. She mouthed syllables like she did when she was trying to tell Andrea a secret she didn't want anyone else to hear. It took Andrea a while before she realized what her mommy was saying. RUN.

Andrea turned and ran back down the hall. She began to sob. The woman was hurting Mommy. She had hurt her daddy bad, and she was going to hurt Andrea too. Behind her she heard a thud and then the sound of something running fast behind her. Andrea looked over her shoulder and saw the scary woman coming for her but running down the hall and dragging her mommy by the throat.

Andrea ran out the open front door, passing her daddy's severed head in the doorway. She screamed as loud as she could and kept screaming until her neighbors in the apartment next door, the Johnsons, opened the door to see what was going on.

Mrs. Johnson was in fuzzy pink pajamas. She held out her arms to Andrea and called her to her, but Andrea kept running for the elevators. She could hear the scary lady behind her. She repeated what her mom had said. "Run!"

Then she heard Mrs. Johnson scream. It was too late.

**17.**

THE ENTIRE building stood swathed in a funereal silence. Dr. David Ebersol stepped out of his rental car and looked up at the brightly lit building, at the amber-tinted windows overlooking Town Lake, behind which some of the wealthiest people in Austin resided. There was no movement inside. It was barely eight o'clock in the evening, yet nothing stirred. There was no movement at all in the monolithic wall of tinted glass. Something was wrong. He could feel it.

Ebersol was staring up at a window on the tenth floor of the building when he saw a lone figure stagger up to the glass and bang on it with both hands. There was something wrong with her that Ebersol could not quite grasp at first. The distance and the dim light backlighting her silhouette obscured her image.

Ebersol gasped in horror as she turned slightly and more of her features became clear. She was naked. There was blood all over her, and one of her breasts was missing. Moments later, the calm, still night exploded with the sound of police sirens and ambulances. Ebersol saw a line of police vehicles making their way down Lamar Boulevard. There were more than half a dozen of them. It was only then that Dr. Ebersol noticed the people huddled across the street. Some were wearing pajamas. There were even a few in their underwear. One or two had spatters of blood on their clothes. They were all staring up at the building, and a few were weeping.

Others appeared to be in shock. A little girl, no more than four or five, sobbed inconsolably and cried out for her mommy, reaching out toward the building.

"Shit!"

Ebersol sprinted into the building, knowing he had to get inside before the police arrived and cordoned it off. He cast one last look up at the window, following the crowd's line of sight. He saw a swift shadow move over the woman and drag her away from the window. Dark liquid spattered the glass as both silhouettes vanished from sight. Ebersol knew in his heart who the shadow was and what she had just done.

On the way here from the airport, Ebersol had stopped to grab two twenty-four-piece buckets of chicken from a fast food place. If Lelani had been hungry enough to eat her fiancé, he knew going in there without food would not be smart. Now he worried that he might be too late to help her. He considered leaving the whole matter to the police, but he knew that would be career suicide. The Aphrodite Aesthetic Reconstruction Clinic had made him famous, and if any connection was made between the clinic and Lelani's rampage, it would make him infamous. He would be a pariah in the industry even if he didn't lose his license. The other issue was his conscience. None of this had been Lelani's fault. He couldn't leave her to take the blame for this mayhem.

He was making his way to the elevator when his cell phone rang.

"Ebersol? It's Trevor. Man, be careful. I was wrong about this thing. Shit is completely fucked over here! Star Mourning—she—she's changed. Her mother called a mental hospital to come get her daughter after she chewed up her own hand and she attacked them. She ate one of the counselors from the mental facility right on her front porch, right in front of me. I don't think we can control this thing by ourselves. I left a message for Sarai, telling her what's going on. She hasn't called back. I don't know what to do, man."

Dr. Ebersol paused. His hand hovered over the elevator call button. What if he couldn't stop Lelani? What if he became her next victim?

"I don't know what to tell you. I've got my own problems over here."

"What's going on? Have you seen Lelani? Has she—you know—changed?"

"I don't know. I just got here. The police are on their way. I think Lelani killed a few people. I don't know. The building looks evacuated, almost. I think I saw her attack someone up there," Ebersol said.

He was hoping the young doctor would tell him what he should do and felt foolish for having such a ridiculous thought. Trevor Adams was no one's savior. He was just a selfish prick who happened to be a genius. As a human being, however, he was an emotional imbecile. That Ebersol was grasping for answers from the same reckless asshole who'd caused all this was a sure sign of his increasing desperation and fear. The reality was, he was on his own here. He took a deep breath and then pushed the elevator button.

"What are you going to do?" Trevor asked. "I mean, what should I do?"

"You need to get that girl sedated and get her to a hospital until we can get her back to the clinic. I'm going up to find Lelani. Keep trying to reach Sarai."

"Oh, uh, okay. I will. Just be careful. Okay? Star—when I saw her attack that guy from the mental hospital—she had claws, man."

"She had what?"

"She had these thick black claws. I think she might have fangs too. She's metamorphosed into some kind of rabid animal. She's taken on some of the physical characteristics of the shrew—claws, red fangs. I think she may even have some kind of neurotoxin in her saliva."

"Have you examined her yet?"

"Uh, um, well, she's still asleep on the front porch. I haven't gone anywhere near her yet. I'm telling you, she slashed one guy's face to ribbons and ripped the other guy apart. I—I'm not going anywhere near her until I get some help."

"So what are you going to do?"

"I called animal control," Trevor answered.

"Who?"

Ebersol was sure he'd heard wrong. The elevator was quickly descending. He could feel his heart rate increase at the thought of ascending into the building. He pressed the button several more times, trying to get the elevator there quickly before the Austin PD invaded the building.

"Animal control. They'll have a tranquilizer guns. I told them there was some kind of large animal out here attacking people. It was a half-truth."

"They're going to call the police the minute they get there if they haven't called them already. You know that, don't you?"

"What else could I do?"

The elevator arrived. When the doors opened, Dr. Ebersol screamed.

Inside the elevator was a slaughterhouse. Blood painted the walls and pooled on the floor an inch thick. What Ebersol could only assume was the woman he'd seen in the window lay in pieces. Her ribcage was completely exposed. Behind it, her heart fibrillated rapidly, the last vestiges of electrochemical activity still trying to restore her heartbeat. But one look at the ruin Lelani had done to the woman's body made it clear that whatever spark of life remained within her flesh would soon be lost to the ether.

Her breasts were completely gone. One of her arms had been wrenched from its socket, and her throat had been savagely mauled. She'd been nearly decapitated. Her head hung precariously from a few masticated tendons.

But that wasn't the worst of the damage. The woman had been gutted. Her torso had been ripped open, and her steaming intestines lay strewn around the elevator. Most of her internal organs were missing, and there was no question in his mind where they had gone.

Lelani stood above the corpse covered in gore from head to toe. Her hair was drenched with blood. Scraps of flesh clung to her face and clothes. She was chewing something. Dr. Ebersol looked down at the pinkish-brown, triangle-shaped organ she held in her hand, trailing two large arteries, and felt bile rise and scald the back of his throat. It was a piece of liver, a human liver. The hand that held it bared little resemblance to a human appendage. From the tips of each finger, knife-like claws as long and thick as the fingers themselves protruded. Blood and saliva drooled from her long crimson canines.

EBERSOL'S legs shook. He felt lightheaded. This was so much more horrible than anything he could have imagined. "Lelani? It's me. It's Dr. Ebersol. It's David."

Lelani's eyes were bloodshot. She looked at him, and for a moment, he saw nothing but hunger in her eyes. Not a hint of recognition. Not a hint of intelligence at all. She brought the bloody organ meat to her mouth and scarfed it down, still staring at Ebersol. He felt his stomach roll and threaten to revolt as he watched her chew the organ she'd ripped from the corpse behind her. The elevator doors began to close and then her eyebrows creased. She tilted her head slightly. She stopped the doors with one lethal-looking hand.

"David?"

"Yes. Yes, it's me."

"I'm so hungry. I'm so hungry, David."

"I know. I know. I'm here to help you. I brought you some food. But we have to get you out of here. Understand? The police are coming. They want to lock you up. You have to come with me."

Ebersol held up the bucket of chicken and wondered if it would be enough. He should have bought a lot more. Her appetite was a lot more than he'd expected. She snatched the bucket of chicken from his hands and began cramming one piece at a time into her mouth.

Going to the rental car was definitely out of the question. The street was slowly filling with police cars. They would be surrounding the building soon, trapping them inside then they'd come in after them.

"Where's the parking garage? Can we get out that way?"

Lelani nodded between bites and then pointed below them. The garage was in the basement. That meant a ride in the elevator. There was no other way. Dr. Ebersol looked around the elevator at the shredded piles of flesh and blood-spattered walls. He steeled his nerves, stepped inside, and blood immediately drenched his Gucci loafers. He kept his eye on how much chicken was left in the bucket, hoping it would last until he could get her out of the building. Six of the twenty pieces were already gone. Lelani had shoved them into her mouth whole and was eating them, bones and all.

"Hurry up! Hurry up!" Ebersol said, punching the down button on the elevator. There were drugs in his car he could use to put her under. Until then, he just had to trust her not to eat him.

**18.** **T**HE FRONT door opened, and Alexis Mourning stepped out with a hypodermic needle. She knelt and quickly injected it into her daughter's arm as the young girl lay sleeping, covered in blood and surrounded by masticated meat. Trevor hesitantly approached.

"Dr. Adams?"

"I got here as quickly as I could. I saw what happened."

"What did you do to my little girl? She's lost her mind!"

"What did you inject her with just now?"

"Ketamine. Dr. Linder brought it with him to sedate her in case she got violent. I can't believe she tore his assistant apart like that. She ate him! Did you see that?"

Trevor nodded. He had seen it all. He was struggling now to keep from going into shock. He and Alexis stared at the corpse. This all seemed so impossible.

"Is that guy okay in there?"

Alexis shook her head.

"He's in bad shape. I think Star punctured his eye and his face."

"Will he live?"

Alexis nodded.

"I think so. He called the police. They'll be here soon. They're going to take my little girl to jail."

"Listen to me, Alexis. I can fix this. I need to get her back to the clinic. Do you understand? That's the only place I can help her. How much ketamine did he bring with him?"

She held up a bottle that contained 500ccs of ketamine. To keep Star unconscious the entire flight, he'd need to dose her with 10 mg an hour. It was enough to do the trick.

"We can take my private jet," Alexis offered. "I'll call ahead."

"Good. That's perfect. I'll get her in the car."

"Dr. Adams? Can I ask you something?" Alexis asked, pausing with the phone in her hand, a worried look on her face.

"Yes, Alexis? We don't have much time. The police will be here any minute."

"I just wanted to ask, after you get her back to the clinic and you cure her, will she still be skinny? I mean, she won't get fat again, will she?"

Dr. Adams's mouth hung open in astonishment. He didn't know how to respond.

On the way to the airport, they passed billboard after billboard along the side of the freeway. There were ads for rum featuring a buxom, scantily clad woman with a dress size smaller than her shoe size. Another ad, for a tropical vacation getaway, showed a woman in a bikini looking out over the ocean as the sun set. The woman had hips narrower than those of a ten-year-old boy. They passed storefronts with mannequins in the window that were all a perfect size three. Even as they hit the off-ramp leading to the airport, billboards for nightclubs, automobiles, even an advertisement for a new housing development all featured women no bigger than the store mannequins.

The last billboard they passed as they turned into the airport parking lot was for a plastic surgery clinic. Not one of the exclusive Beverly Hills clinics he'd always dreamed of working in before being recruited by the Aphrodite Aesthetic Reconstruction Clinic. This was one of those chain operations that did boob jobs for four thousand dollars a pop. The woman on the poster looked like a Barbie doll. She had an impossibly small, Photoshopped waist and breasts so large they threatened to snap that twenty-inch waist in half from the sheer force of gravity. It was an impossible aesthetic ideal and one that he had promoted, his entire industry had promoted. He turned away and saw hotel ads featuring happy couples, all slender and fit, not a single indication of America's obesity epidemic. It was all an illusion, and people were dying for it.

"Where's your plane?"

"It's over there, but we have to go through customs."

"Not yet we don't. We're not taking your plane to Cancun. We're flying to Florida. We'll switch planes there and fly in on the clinic's private airplane. It'll be less suspicious having an unconscious girl strapped to a gurney with tubes sticking out of her if we're flying to a medical facility. Besides, there's medical equipment on the clinic's jet we can use to keep her stabilized."

Trevor rolled up her sleeves and gave her another shot, easing the needle into one of the throbbing blue veins that now crisscrossed her emaciated body like worms crawling under her skin. She barely stirred.

"Let's go."

VER SINCE his kidney transplant, Jeffrey felt like a new man. After more than a year on the transplant list, he'd almost given up hope, and then some rich bastard gets annihilated by a police car and Jeffrey gets a new lease on life. It was funny how karma worked sometimes.

Jeffrey had lost a ton of weight in the last few days. He looked absolutely fabulous. He wasn't just skinny, he was "gay skinny," which was just a couple pounds shy of "prison-camp skinny." He posed in the mirror, wearing a pair of skinny jeans and a tight, gray, fashionably vintage v-neck T-shirt. His life would be perfect if it wasn't for his insane hunger.

Tonight, he was going to Club X to pick up some "man pussy," as he liked to call it. Jeffrey didn't think of himself as gay or bisexual. He hated labels. Jeffrey just liked to fuck, and his tastes varied from day to day. Fucking a guy one day and a woman the next was no different to him then dating a tall chick and then dating a short chick. He just wasn't into limiting his sexual choices. He knew how that infuriated gays and straights alike, but Jeffrey didn't give a fuck. Cock or pussy, it just didn't matter when his dick was hard, but tonight, he definitely wanted some ass. There was no way he was going to let his new svelte physique go to waste.

He stopped at a drive-through taco place on the way and ordered a burrito. He had been eating every hour or so, since the surgery. His appetite was out of control, but for some reason it didn't seem to be affecting his weight at all. He chalked it up to the anti-rejection medication. It must have been reacting with his HIV meds somehow. At least he didn't need weed anymore to give him an appetite. That shit was expensive, and anyone who said it wasn't addictive was a goddamn liar. As fierce as the munchies were, though, they weren't shit compared to what he felt now. He was absolutely voracious. For once, his appetite for food almost matched his appetite for sex. Almost.

It had only been six days since the surgery, and the doctor said he wasn't supposed to do anything vigorous for four to six weeks, but there was no way Jeffrey was going to go without sex for a month. That just wasn't happening. He still felt tired, and there was a little pain in his side from the surgery, but the meds were awesome. The worst part was having to take a cab everywhere, but that was the one piece of advice the doctor gave him that he did heed. No driving for six to eight weeks. He needed to find him a boyfriend or some lonely MILF to drive him around. He couldn't afford taxis every night on unemployment.

The taxi driver was a Muslim guy in a turban who looked like he'd stepped right out of a Bollywood feature. He wasn't bad looking. He had almond-shaped eyes and dark tan skin, bow-shaped lips that were almost womanly. He was a little prettier than the manly men Jeffrey preferred, and the guy made him nervous. He kept glancing back at Jeffrey and smiling, trying to make awkward conversation. Jeffrey knew these Muslim guys hated gays. They hung them in Saudi Arabia, he'd heard. But this was America, so fuck him.

"You going to that club on Fourth Street? Harry's?"

"No, that place is for fags. I'm going to The Cocktail, where all the refined homosexuals hang out," Jeffrey answered snidely, and then turned to stare out the window at the skyline as they crawled through traffic on I-35. He was trying to offend the man enough to shut him the fuck up, but it wasn't working. The guy just persisted with his stupid questions.

"You think a guy like me would like that club?"

Jeffrey rolled his eyes.

"No, I don't think it would be your cup of tea."

"I'm from Afghanistan. They don't have clubs like this there."

"No, I wouldn't imagine they would." Jeffrey sighed impatiently. He was getting hungry again and sleepy and irritated. He just wanted to eat, get a blowjob, and go to sleep. If he got lucky, maybe he'd get a blowjob while eating. He imagined a big, fat T-bone steak and a big, strong blue-collar man, maybe even a cowboy. That would be the perfect evening.

"Maybe you could take me there sometime?"

Jeffrey felt like an ass. The guy was gay. This was probably his first "out-of-the-closet" moment, and Jeffrey had almost brushed him off. Jeffrey remembered the first person he came out to. It was his Spanish teacher, Mr. Villaria. Jeffrey was only fifteen years old. There had been rumors about Mr. Villaria being spotted holding hands with guys and hanging out at gay clubs on Fourth Street, so Jeffrey had rolled the dice and opened up to the man. He'd secretly hoped Mr. Villaria would sweep him into his arms and make mad passionate love to him right there in the classroom.

What his teacher did instead was much cooler. He sat Jeffrey down and warned him about older men who use young boys like him. He told him about safe sex and steered him toward a few GLBT youth groups in the area, and finally he'd told him to always be proud of who he was and never let anyone make him feel ashamed for being gay. He even offered to call a meeting with his parents here at the school if Jeffrey was worried about how they would react to the news. His "coming-out" experience had been cooler than almost anyone he knew.

He'd heard all the horror stories about being laughed at, beaten up, kicked out of the house. He hadn't gone through any of that.

He also didn't listen to much of his teacher's advice about safe sex or avoiding older men, but that had been his own damn stupid fault. Mr. Villaria had been amazing. Jeffrey, on the other hand, had almost told this guy to fuck off.

"What's your name?"

"Ajani."

"Ajani? My name's Jeffrey. I'll tell you what, I'm starving. You take me to get something to eat and turn that meter off, and I'll give you a night you won't forget."

Ajani smiled broadly.

"What do you want to eat?"

"I'm in the mood for a steak."

In the back of the cab, in the parking lot of Simone's Steakhouse, Ajani moaned and sighed as Jeffrey thrust deep into his virgin ass. He reached around and stroked Ajani off just as he erupted in the young Arab's lubricated rectum, filling it with his seed. It had felt so good.

That's when Jeffrey realized it had felt too good. He slid his lubricated cock out of Ajani's ass and gasped at the sight of the shredded latex curled up like a cock ring at the base of his erection.

"Oh, fuck. Oh, shit."

"What's wrong?" Ajani asked, still panting. His face appeared elated, like he was having the time of his life.

Jeffrey almost felt bad telling him the bad news.

"I think we have a big problem."

That night, Ajani went home with two diseases. The genetic retrovirus created by Dr. Trevor Adams piggybacked onto the HIV virus, using the virus to carry pygmy shrew DNA from Jeffrey to Ajani in a few brief thrusts of Jeffrey's cock into Ajani's ecstatically receptive virgin anus. Over the next few weeks, Ajani's increasingly popular asshole would spread the virus up and down Fourth Street. Within a month, it had spread to the heterosexual community.

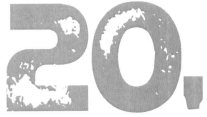

THE GREASY, fatty, high-calorie fried meat tasted good. It was warm and soothing. The surge of calories quieted Lelani's hunger. She stared at the face of the man who'd brought her the food and tried hard to remember who he was. She had known his name just a second ago and then the hunger had resurfaced and obliterated all recollection. He had interrupted her meal but had provided her with another. Now the hunger had been momentarily quelled. She was feeling sleepy again. She'd burned so many calories hunting down prey, and she'd consumed so many more from the people she'd killed. Her stomach felt bloated. She needed to rest, to recover.

The memory of murdering and eating her neighbors caused only the slightest pang of remorse. It had been necessary. They had the calories she needed to survive. Killing and eating them was no different than slaughtering a cow for beef or hunting deer for venison. It was a biological imperative. If she didn't eat, she would die, and there were no cows in downtown Austin, but there were plenty of people, and human flesh contained enough calories to sustain her for hours.

"David. Dr. David Ebersol," Lelani said between bites. She looked at David Ebersol and saw the succulent flesh, the smooth, supple skin, the jiggle of fat around his waist and neck. Her mouth began to water.

"Yes, Lelani. It's me. I'm here to help you," Ebersol said as he pounded on the elevator button, urgently pressing the one that took them to the basement.

"Help me?" Lelani asked, tilting her head slightly in a way that made her look even more animalistic, like a feral dog examining some strange prey it had never encountered before, trying to decide if it was dangerous or something else it could kill and eat. She knew Dr. Ebersol was here to help her. Somewhere deep in her unconscious mind she knew there was danger around. People were coming to hurt her. People were chasing them. Police. Police were coming to arrest her because she'd eaten people. She felt a brief moment of revulsion followed immediately by the most profound sensory recall. She remembered how delicious it had all tasted. How good it felt to feel their life forces fill her belly. The taste had been like warm sushi with a pulse. The fatty meat melted like butter on her tongue. She closed her eyes and shuddered at the memory.

"Yes. I'm going to get you out of here. Get you back to the clinic and get you back to normal."

"I need food."

"I know. There's more food in the car. We just have to get you there. There's police all over the building. We need to get past them to get to the food."

Lelani bared her teeth and raised one of her taloned hands so Ebersol could see them. It was coated with gore and chicken grease.

"I'll kill them!"

"No. We can't kill anyone else, Lelani. They have guns. They'll hurt you."

As powerful as Lelani's hunger was, her survival instinct was just as powerful. "Okay, David."

"I'll feed you. I'll help you, but no more killing. Understand?"

"Okay, David," Lelani replied, nodding as she crammed another chicken breast into her mouth and crunched it between her serrated teeth.

Lelani felt the sensation of falling and remembered she was in an elevator. There were people chasing them. People with guns. Lelani was barely conscious of the danger. The hunger made it so hard to concentrate on anything, but the chicken had helped. It had soothed the maddening ravenousness for a while.

David said the police would try to hurt her, lock her away, but he didn't want her to kill them. She could do it easily. She could open up their fat bellies with one swipe of her claws, tear out their throats with her fangs. The thought was empowering. It was better than being onstage and hearing the crowd applaud as she pranced like a show pony in clothes designed to make women feel ugly without them and like royalty if they were one of the lucky few who could actually afford them. She had thought being desired by men and envied by women was power, but this was real power—the ability to take a life with ease, to inspire fear. She smiled as she chewed up another piece of fried chicken and reached into the bucket for more. She wasn't hungry anymore, but the food was there, so she continued to eat. What she really needed was sleep, but they had to get away first.

The elevator doors opened, and they stepped out into the nearly empty parking garage. The concrete structure was well lit, and security cameras were affixed to the thick pillars that held up the ceilings. The parking garage itself was two stories, buried below street level beneath the building. A steel gate with a digital keypad protected the garage from unauthorized entry, and a guard was usually posted there as well. But Lelani had already murdered the guard when someone had called him to help after Lelani had broken into her neighbor's apartment and torn him apart. She'd done the same to the armed guard, ripping his corpulent belly open and pulling out his steaming insides, stuffing his wet squishy organs into her mouth by the fistfuls before he could get his gun out of the holster. She ate his liver in front of him while he watched, dying. The liver was full of calories and nutrients, but she'd always hated liver before the treatment. Her mother used to make her eat liver and onions as a kid. She'd have to sit at the table, long after everyone else had finished and were in the kitchen watching television, until she finished her plate. But this time she had scarfed it down in a few quick bites and then yanked out his pancreas and ate that as well, followed by his heart. They were all delicious.

"This way," Ebersol whispered, taking Lelani by the arm and leading her across the parking garage.

His car was still on the street, and getting to it would mean going through cops, if they were already circling around to the back of the building as he suspected. Still, getting out of the parking garage and on to the street was their only chance at escaping.

"We need to run. Maybe they haven't gotten back here yet."

They sprinted toward the exit, reaching it just as two police officers stepped through. Dr. Ebersol threw his hands up in surrender. Lelani slashed a claw across the face of the first officer through the exit door, cutting his cheek down to the bone, puncturing his left eye and gouging it from the socket. It drooled down his face, dangling from the ocular nerves like a dead jellyfish.

The officer, a kid no more than twenty-five, fell to the floor screaming.

"My eye! My fucking eye!"

The next officer almost got his gun out of the holster before she leaped into his arms and bit down on his nose, crunching through the cartilage like a dry chicken bone and tearing it off his face, leaving a ragged crater. He cried out for help as she slashed her claws across his face, silencing him as she rode the balding, fat, middle-aged police officer down to the concrete. She slashed and ripped at him, tearing open his chest and throat, rending his face to ribbons before Ebersol grabbed her and pulled her out the door.

The cop with the missing eye was still crying out, and he was going for his radio. Lelani dived on top of him and seized his throat between her jaws. With a single jerk of her head, she tore out his trachea. The arterial spray saturated her hair and clothes and misted the exit door behind her. She paused to grab the bucket of chicken before she followed Dr. Ebersol out into the night. The exertion had made her hungry again. She was still chewing on the flesh she'd torn from the young officer's throat when she shoved another piece of chicken into her mouth.

"Come on! The other cops might have heard their screams. We need to get to my car!"

They jogged out into the night. Gardens surrounded the property, and beyond that, just over a low stone wall, was the jogging path that circled Town Lake.

"Go down to the lake. I'll get my car and meet you at the dog park on Congress Avenue. Do you understand?"

Lelani nodded and picked up another piece of chicken and shoved it into her mouth.

Ebersol looked into the bucket and she did the same. Only two pieces left. She saw the worried expression on his face when he looked back up at her.

"I've got more in my car. Don't hurt anyone else while you're waiting for me. I'll be there right away, okay?"

"I'm so hungry, David. I'm so hungry," Lelani said, shaking her head.

"Please, Lelani. I promise. I'll help you, but you can't keep killing people."

The problem was, she was beginning to enjoy killing. Fried chicken didn't fight back. It didn't scream. It didn't fear her. Fried chicken just wasn't as much fun.

POLICE WERE every-where. It took Dr. Ebersol nearly twenty minutes to get to his car and then to navigate through the throngs of gawkers and curiosity seekers onto Congress Avenue and down to the lake.

The dog park was a large open area beside the lake, just under the Congress Street bridge. There was little grass left that hadn't been trampled and pissed on until it had shriveled up, leaving large brown patches and even larger areas where there was no grass at all. He found Lelani asleep in the dirt, alone, shivering like a dope fiend in detox. The empty paper bucket had been ripped to confetti and littered the ground around her. Her huge claws were caked with blood. Her mouth hung open, revealing blood-stained fangs. She was naked, and her body was little more than a collection of bones, like a feral dog someone had shaved bald.

Ebersol left the car running as he walked over and lifted Lelani into his arms. She weighed less than his ten-year-old niece, seventy or eighty pounds at most. It was like lifting a papier-mâché Halloween scarecrow. He was certain he could crush her waifish body with ease if it wasn't for the fangs and claws. She stirred slightly but did not wake while he carried her back to his vehicle. Her skin was as hot as asphalt in August. Ebersol began to sweat as he carried her across the park to his waiting car. Her heartbeat thundered against his chest. It was well more than a hundred beats per minute. It was the pulse of someone running a sprint, not someone in a deep sleep.

Ebersol felt his testicles shrivel up against him when Lelani nuzzled her face in the crook of his neck, making a growling, purring sound. A chill shivered up his spine. If she woke up hungry while he was still carrying her, Ebersol knew he was completely fucked. They made it to the car without incident, and Ebersol drove her to the airport. Sarai had arranged for the clinic's private jet to meet them.

**T**AMMY WAS still hungry when her mother put her to bed. She wore her eye patch just as Dr. Savaresse had instructed her to do and crawled beneath the covers. Her mom and dad kissed her good night. Her mother had just gotten out of the shower, and the smell of her clean skin made Tammy's mouth water. Her stomach growled. It felt like it was eating itself.

"Can I have a snack before bedtime?"

Her father shook his head. "You've been eating all day, sweetie. Enough's enough. We'll make you a nice breakfast in the morning. Okay?"

Tammy shook her head. "No! I need to eat now! I'm hungry now!"

Her head whipped sideways and her left cheek sang out in pain. Her father had slapped her across the face. The blow made her new eyes throb, and she hoped he hadn't damaged them.

"You watch your damned mouth, young lady! You will eat when I say you can eat! Do you understand?"

Her father was a big, barrel-chested man. He was tall and broad-shouldered, with hands like catcher's mitts. His red hair and beard made him look like a lumberjack in a business suit. Tammy thought he looked like the Greek god Zeus, only with red hair. His voice was deep but powerful. It boomed like thunder when he was agitated or excited.

Tammy began to cry. It wasn't the pain of her father's blow but the hunger clawing through her guts that hurt so much more. "I'm hungry, Daddy!"

"You'll eat in the morning!" He stormed out of the room and slammed the door, dragging Tammy's mother out with him.

Tammy could still hear them arguing about her in the hallway. It was nothing new. They argued every night, and if Tammy wasn't the cause of the argument, her name was usually dragged into it at some point.

"Maybe there's something wrong with her. It might have something to do with the medications she's on for the pain and the anti-rejection medications. She has lost an awful lot of weight."

"There's nothing wrong with that damn kid. The doctor would have told us if there was something wrong. She's just spoiled."

"Not by you, she isn't. You couldn't even come to the hospital the day your daughter saw for the first time in her life!"

"I had to work! If I wasn't out there busting my hump, you wouldn't be able to stay home and spoil her rotten the way you do!"

"I'm going to look up the symptoms of those medications on the Internet. I'm telling you, something's wrong with her."

"So, no sex tonight again?"

"You've got a hand."

Tammy tossed and turned, unable to sleep. She'd never been this hungry in her life. She moaned and whined, kicked her covers off, then pulled them back up and wrapped them around herself, and then kicked them off again. She was hot. It felt like she was burning up from the inside. Sweat bulleted down her face, soaking her pajamas and sheets.

Tammy called out to her parents. "Can I get some water?"

"No! You'll wet the bed!"

Tammy was almost nine. She hadn't wet the bed in months. She climbed out of bed and began to pace. She could still hear her parents arguing down the hall behind their bedroom door, but she could no longer make out what they were saying. All she had to do is wait until they fell asleep and she could raid the refrigerator. It wouldn't be long now. They would get tired of hating each other soon.

It was after midnight when Tammy's parents finally fell asleep. Tammy was starving by then. Her stomach was in knots. Her mouth hurt. Her teeth felt too big, and they kept cutting her lip. The blood tasted so good she started doing it on purpose, biting into her bottom lip just to taste something, anything. Her hands were different too. Her nails had grown. They were dark and ugly, like a witch's. She was turning into a monster. Everything would be all right as soon as she got something to eat. She could feel it.

Tammy couldn't wait any longer. She opened her door and crept down the hall on her tiptoes. She raised her eye patch but resisted the urge to turn on the lights. The night was crushing down on her from all sides. She felt like Pinocchio's Papa Geppetto creeping through the belly of a whale—the way she'd felt when she'd first lost her eyesight. But she knew her way around the house. Four years of blindness had made her accustomed to the night.

Deftly, Tammy avoided the living room couch, the floor lamp, the coffee table, the bookcase with the leather-bound first editions that nobody read, and the china hutch filled with dishware they'd never used. She crept into the kitchen and opened the refrigerator. She was salivating profusely, and her stomach was in agony. There was no way to avoid the little light in the fridge. If her parents were really asleep it wouldn't matter, and if they weren't, they would hear her anyway.

Tammy groped around the refrigerator. Her eyesight was still fuzzy, and she was accustomed to relying more on her other senses. She grabbed a doggie bag her parents brought home from a restaurant they'd gone to while she was still in the hospital, and she sniffed it. There was a piece of lamb with mint jelly, wasabi mashed potatoes, and green beans and baby carrots. She tipped the bag up and dumped its contents into her mouth. She quickly chewed it up and reached back into the fridge, feeling around until her fingers landed on her mother's Greek yogurt. She ripped off the lid and scooped it out with her fingers. She'd eaten half the cup when she heard the heavy footsteps behind her.

Someone grabbed her from behind and jerked her to the floor. "What the fuck are you doing out of bed?"

The cup of yogurt splattered across the floor. Tammy lifted her eye patch and stared down at the milky curds smeared across the tiles. Her stomach growled, and then she growled as well. Without thinking, she bit the hand that held her down, gouging her teeth deep into the skin and crunching down on her father's thick phalanges. A finger came off in her mouth and she chewed it absentmindedly as her father began to scream.

A blow struck the side of her head, and everything went fuzzy and dark and stayed that way. One of her new corneas had detached. It didn't matter; she could hear her father's cries, smell the sweaty, pissy stench of his fear. He was curled into a ball, moaning, whimpering, and crying out in pain. Tammy still had his finger in her mouth, crunching it up with jaws grown enormously powerful overnight. It didn't taste bad. In fact, to her, it tasted as delicious as the lamb had moments ago.

Her father's thrashing began to subside as the neurotoxin in Tammy's saliva hit his nervous system, causing his muscles to seize. He grunted a few times, quivering and convulsing but unable to move. And Tammy was still hungry.

"Bill? Bill?"

Tammy's mother ran down the hall in a cloud of perfume, panic, and hairspray. Tammy didn't want to hurt her mother, but she didn't want to relinquish her new meal either, and she'd defend it if she had to.

"Oh, my God! What are you doing?" Her mother ran over to her and tried to pry Tammy off her father's chest. Tammy had eaten his trapezius muscle, chewed her way from the base of his neck down to his shoulder blade. The plate-shaped bone was clean of flesh. It glistened in the light of the open refrigerator door.

Tammy's mother screamed and violently shook her. "What did you do? What did you do? Why?"

Her father trembled beneath her as he bled out from the ragged hole in his back and neck, going into shock.

Tammy shrugged.

"I told you I was hungry, Mommy."

She continued her meal as her mother fainted, smacking her head on the granite countertop on the way to the floor. She would never awaken from the blow. In a few hours, Tammy would begin eating her mother as well. When they were both gone, the obese pederast next door was next. He'd touched her butt once and tried to shove her hand down his pants. Then he'd masturbated in front of her, thinking she wouldn't know it was him because she couldn't see. But she had known it was him, even though he didn't say a word. She could smell his sweaty bacon and cheese scent and hear his labored, congested breathing, lungs suffocating beneath layers of blubbery fat. She licked her lips, thinking of all the delicious calories in that corpulent mountain of useless meat and tissue.

23.

DR. SARAI Mahendru waited in the limousine at Cancun International Airport outside the private aviation terminal. In moments, her two most valuable doctors were due to arrive from their ordeal. Ever since she'd received their frantic back-to-back messages, she'd been obsessing over their dilemma. Two of the fourteen patients they'd treated in the last week had descended into madness and cannibalism. Her staff was now in the process of contacting the other twelve. One of them had died in an automobile accident, which presented a host of other issues. He'd been an organ donor and his organs and tissue had now gone out to more than eighteen people and could go to as many as thirty more. If those organs and tissue contained Dr. Trevor Adam's retrovirus, there was no telling how many people were now infected. She needed help fixing this, and it had to be someone she trusted.

She'd called an old acquaintance from her days at Harvard Medical School, Professor Ryan Vivaan. He'd been a graduate student like her when she'd first made his acquaintance back in '98. Now he worked for India's Ministry of Science and Technology in their genetic research facility. Before she'd discovered Dr. Trevor Adams, she'd been courting Professor Vivaan to join the clinic. He'd refused, citing ethical concerns. Convincing him to help rescue the clinic from the consequences of the very same ethical concerns he'd worried about had not been easy.

"Ryan? This is Sarai Mahendru. Do you have a moment?"

Though Sarai's father was Indian, she had never learned the language, a fact that annoyed her father not nearly as much as it seemed to annoy Professor Vivaan. She could hear him let out a heavy sigh from the other end of the phone. Breathing heavy and rolling his eyes, as if the totality of life were one massive inconvenience was one of his more endearing character traits.

"I am very busy, Sarai. What can I do for you? Is this about risking my reputation by injecting fat, lazy, unhealthy Americans with DNA to make them look like they would if they ate properly and exercised?"

Sarai sighed. "Ryan, this is serious. I need your help. We have made some … mistakes. You were right."

There was a long pause.

"Ryan?"

"I'm trying to decide if I should hang up before I get drawn into whatever madness you've created over there."

"I'll pay you twice your annual salary for one month of your time."

"Two weeks, and I can back out at any time."

"Okay, but I need you on a plane today."

"Why so urgent?"

"I'll explain everything when you get here."

"Is this as bad as it sounds?"

"It's worse. Much worse." Sarai hung up.

Minutes later, the clinic's private Gulfstream G-550 touched down. She felt a flutter in her stomach. Usually, the G-550 was reserved for their very wealthiest clients, though many of them preferred to use their own jets. Today it carried something terrifying, something Sarai could scarcely imagine.

It had been more than a decade since Sarai borrowed the hundred million from her family and various banks to convert the old Spanish hotel into a world-class medical resort. Then she was one of the world's leading plastic surgeons. Now she was a bureaucrat who spent more time behind a computer than using a scalpel. After opening this place, she'd discovered that her greatest gift was her ability to recognize talent. Sarai lured Dr. David Ebersol to the clinic from his posh Beverly Hills facility by offering him a tenth of the profits in addition to his considerable salary, and with him, she'd gotten all his famous and affluent clients. Once they experienced recovering from surgery in a beachfront resort with a butler service, five-star meals prepared by their own personal chef, and served on fine china with real silverware, personal massages, in-room pool and Jacuzzi, word of mouth did the rest. It wasn't long before the Aphrodite Aesthetic Reconstruction Clinic was bringing in hundreds of millions a year. Now it was all in jeopardy.

Sarai watched as two gurneys were carried off the plane, followed by the two doctors. She took a deep breath and stepped out of the limo. Two ambulances were parked on the runway. Sarai waved them over. The EMTs rushed to take charge of the two high-profile patients. Dr. Ebersol walked down the runway behind the gurney carrying Lelani. His expression was stoic, but Sarai had known him long enough to recognize the pain and anger roiling inside him. Only now did it occur to her that the man was in love with Lelani.

Trevor Adams stumbled down the runway in a loping, intoxicated swagger, wearing an expression of depression and defeat that made Sarai want to slap him sober. There was no time for anyone to check out, least of all the one responsible for the mess in the first place, though Sarai took her share of responsibility.

It had been her idea to recruit a geneticist. Sarai had seen it as the next logical step in the evolution of cosmetic medicine. And she knew the reputation of young Dr. Adams when she'd recruited him. His recklessness and willingness to break laws had been as big a selling point as his considerable genius. In hindsight, that had been a careless mistake on her part. She had to live with that mistake now.

She had pushed him to produce a new treatment they could market exclusively, and he had done precisely that. What he created was amazing. Sarai had been so impressed, she'd begun advertising it before animal trials were complete. The clinic booked the first twenty reservations for the new treatment before the first human trials had even begun. The new treatment had promised to make them all millions. Sarai watched as the results of her impetuousness was wheeled down the runway to the ambulance.

The woman was practically a corpse. There was no meat on her at all, just bones, thinly veiled in skin. Muscle and adipose tissue had been burned away by a metabolism that was clearly out of control. The girl's bird-like chest rose and fell rapidly as she panted in a fitful narcotic-induced slumber. The girl's heart pounded against her fragile ribcage. That the girl was still alive was a marvel. Her body was eating itself. It had devoured every ounce of subcutaneous tissue and was now cannibalizing her organs. There was little doubt in Sarai's mind that the girl was dying.

Sarai took a deep breath and was surprised to feel tears in her eyes. She reached out and stroked the girl's forehead. The skin was hot to the touch. She took her hand and gently squeezed. The fingers were gnarled like tree roots, as if afflicted with severe arthritis. They curled inward. The nails had grown long and thick and sharp, more claws than fingers. They were coated with flecks of dried blood. The girl's other hand was wrapped in bandages. Sarai patted the back of her hand and laid it back on the gurney. She took a deep breath and wiped a tear from her eye. She hoped she hadn't ruined this girl's life forever. There was no telling what emotional scars she would have. Sarai could not imagine living with the knowledge that you'd murdered someone for no reason, just to appease your hunger, eaten someone alive. It was going to be hard enough for Sarai to live with the fact that it had been her fault. She looked from the girl's gruesomely emaciated near-carcass into Dr. Trevor Adam's bloodshot eyes.

"Are you satisfied?" she asked. Trevor looked away. "You stay right there with her all the way to the clinic, and if she dies, you contact her mother. Understand?"

"She's behind us," Trevor answered.

Sarai looked up, and sure enough, she recognized the still amazingly beautiful face of one of the world's most recognizable actresses, Alexis Mourning. The woman looked perfectly put together, not so much as an eyelash out of place. The streaks of black tears and smeared mascara one would typically expect to see on a woman whose child was dying were nowhere to be found. Alexis was staring into a mirror and liberally applying powder as she tipped along in impossibly high shoes. She looked up, realized she had fallen behind her daughter, tucked the mirror and powder away, tilted her chin skyward, and increased her pace to catch up.

Sarai shook her head. With effort, she wrestled the expression of disgust and disdain from her face, plastered on a smile, and then thought better of it and changed it to something more solemn and compassionate.

She stepped forward and offered her hand to Alexis. "I'm so sorry about all of this. Don't worry, we'll do everything we can for her. I have some of the best doctors in the world on their way to help, as you know, we have one of the best medical and research facilities on the planet here at the clinic."

Alexis nodded. It was obvious to Sarai that Alexis was fighting with something. There was something she wanted to say but couldn't quite find the right words.

"Yes, Ms. Mourning? You have a question?"

"What—what's wrong with her? Why did she go crazy like that? She—she ate all the food in the refrigerator. I have a Sub Zero, like the kind they have in restaurants. You can almost walk into it. She emptied it in a couple hours. Then she—oh my God! She ate someone! What did you do to her?"

Sarai maintained her stoic expression. She looked directly into Alexis's eyes as the woman spoke as if she were hanging on every one of the famous actress's words. She placed a consoling hand on Alexis's shoulder. "Mrs. Mourning, your daughter is having a reaction to the treatment. She's losing too much weight. In essence, she's starving to death. We're feeding her intravenously to keep her alive until we can reverse the effects."

"I don't understand. How can she be starving after all the food she ate?"

"The calories she's eating are being burned up faster than she can consume them. Her body is instantly converting the calories into a coenzyme called ATP before it can be stored as fat, and her muscles are using that ATP as fast as it is being produced."

"So she can never get fat?"

"No. That's what the treatment was for."

"Then it worked, right? I mean, if she can't get fat, then the treatment worked?" Alexis seemed elated. Her daughter was dying right before her eyes, reduced to skin and bones, and her mother only appeared concerned with how much weight she'd lost. The actress paused again, obviously thinking deeply about something.

"Yes?"

"I asked Dr. Adams if—I mean, when they cure Star, will she get fat again?"

Sarai tried and failed to hide her astonishment. She slowly shook her head. "I—I don't know."

"If she gets fat again, I want my money back, every penny of it! You understand?"

"Yes. Yes, of course."

"One more thing," Alexis said. She looked around and then looked down at the ground in an uncharacteristic show of insecurity.

Finally she leaned in close and cupped a hand over her mouth so she could whisper in Sarai's ear. "If it works. I mean—if you can fix it—I want you to do it to me, okay?"

Sarai leaned away. She practically recoiled. This time there was no disguising her contempt, but Alexis appeared either to not care or not notice. Sarai regained her composure.

"Yes, of course. Whatever you wish, ma'am."

The EMTs lifted Star into the ambulance, and Trevor climbed inside with her. Sarai began walking back toward the limousine. She heard heels clicking behind her. She turned and was surprised to see Alexis keeping pace with her.

"Don't you want to ride with your daughter in the ambulance?"

"You didn't bring a limo for me?"

Sarai smiled wide, a big, artificial widening of the lips to hide her increasing revulsion toward the woman. "Yes, of course. You can take mine."

**A**T THE clinic, more bad news awaited Dr. Sarai Mahendru. Her staff had located the other twelve patients, and the news wasn't good. Three of their patients were in the news this morning, causing a firestorm of rumor and speculation. Was it a new drug a lethal side-effect? Bath salts? A satanic cult? Zombie virus? Star Mourning's mauling of the two guys from the psychiatric hospital had not gone unnoticed by the media. The survivor was telling a reporter about Alexis Mourning running off with her daughter and some mysterious man without waiting for the police. Now there was a warrant out for both of them.

Earlier that day there had been replays of the now-infamous on-air attack of Samuel "Big Easy" Saldeine upon his producer. Sarai watched it once, just long enough to see Big Easy munching on his producer's entrails like links of Polish sausage. The attack had been broadcast live into tens of millions of households. He had eaten the man alive. The police were launching an investigation, starting with a thorough autopsy. The autopsy worried Sarai the most. If they noticed the genetic changes, it wouldn't be long before they traced it back to the clinic.

The worst of the reports involved Nathan Gingred, a former US congressman and one-time presidential candidate who now stood accused of cannibalizing his own children, including his eight-month-old son.

Sarai knew she had to keep that last detail from Professor Vivaan. If he found out about it, he would bolt, wash his hands of all of this, and they needed his expertise in order to find a cure. They had located most of the other patients. Three of them were already dead, six more were on their way to the clinic, Big Easy was in police custody pending trial for eating his producer, and Star Mourning and Lelani Simms were already at the clinic. Only the congressman was missing. He had taken off after eating his kids, and no one could find him. Then there was the matter of the transplant recipients. That had been bugging Sarai.

There had been other bizarre incidents of spontaneous cannibalism in the news. A basketball player had eaten an orderly at a hospital in Austin. A little girl had eaten both her parents in the same city, and there had been random attacks at several gay clubs in the area. All in the same city where the chef, one of their patients, had died in a car accident and his organs had been harvested for transplant.

"Shit." Sarai punched her desk, cutting the skin on her knuckles and drawing blood but not appearing to notice as she stared out the window at the waves crashing against the beach and all the happy beachgoers splashing about in the water or sunbathing on the beach. *My life should be so simple*, she thought.

Initial tests of the two patients they'd brought in yesterday revealed startling physiological changes. Their bodies were burning calories at an extraordinary rate, thousands of calories an hour, and there were more than ten times the normal levels of adrenaline in their bloodstream. Trevor had done more than accelerated their metabolism, he'd set off a firestorm in the rage centers of their brains.

PET scans of Star Mourning's amygdala showed increased blood flow to the frontal lobe. Blood tests revealed infinitesimal levels of acetylcholine, a hormone that tempers the more severe effects of adrenalin, and monoamine oxidase A, a hormone that break down dopamine and other monoamine neurotransmitters such as serotonin and norepinephrine, critical for impulse control and modulating emotional responses. What the tests revealed was someone with a raging appetite, a nervous system excited by an overdose of adrenaline mimicking extreme rage, and no impulse control, no ability to regulate or suppress this hormonal onslaught.

Like a pubescent teenager on crack.

Even more startling were the physical changes. The entire structure of Star's jaw had changed. It had elongated and thickened. The incisors had lengthened and shifted forward, and a red coloring on the tips had been caused by the accumulation of some kind of iron ore. Samples of Star's saliva contained a neurotoxin that blocks the interaction of neurons with neurotransmitters, making it impossible for them to receive signals, impairing nerve function and causing painful paralysis of the muscles and even destroying neurons and causing permanent cell damage. It was an effective weapon. It would render victims helpless with one bite, immobilizing them while they were eaten alive.

Even Star's hands had changed. They were thick and knobby with knife-like claws extending from the fingertips. The claws were deadly sharp. Sarai shuddered, imagining those claws ripping open someone's chest.

Sarai called Drs. Adams, Ebersol, and Vivaan into her office. She stared out the window again before turning on her computer. The first thing she saw was a headline about a sexually transmitted virus that was turning people into cannibals.

Sexually transmitted? The virus had mutated, become infectious. Everything had just become a little more complicated. Doctors from the Centers for Disease Control linked the virus to several gay clubs in downtown Austin. The virus had taken on a street name—"Skinny"—and once the media reported it, the disease became a craze. People were deliberately getting themselves infected in order to lose weight. The CDC named the illness AHMS (Acquired

Hyper-Metabolism Syndrome), and they were hard at work tracking down the disease's origin, looking for "Patient Zero." So far, they had identified a young bisexual man who'd recently died of the disease. He was HIV positive and they were proceeding under the hypothesis that the HIV virus had somehow mutated.

Despite reports of shut-ins cooking and eating their pets, people robbing supermarkets for food, gorging themselves at buffets and fast food restaurants, and even resorting to cannibalizing their young and elderly, all anyone in the public heard was that those afflicted with the virus had achieved the ideal American aesthetic. They were skinny. No exercise. No diet. It was the perfect weight-loss miracle. It just happened to turn people into psychopaths.

Facebook and Twitter were abuzz with talk of the disease:

"I would totally love to get that disease. My cousin got it and lost seventy pounds in one week!"

"Didn't she eat her grandma though?"

"Yeah, but it was totally worth it if you ask me. Her grandma was old anyway and that bitch was fat as hell!"

"Did you hear about that new disease that makes people skinny? I wish I had it. I could stand to lose a few pounds. LOL."

"Stock your fridge and then go out and get your fat ass infected! Quick and easy cure for the epidemic of American obesity. LMAO!"

"It would fix the economy too. I'm buying stock in McDonald's! ROFL!"

Sarai clicked on a news article about a prostitute who'd been burned in a fire and received a skin graft. She'd been caught with the cannibalized bodies of a dozen tricks in her basement. Below that was a story about a cab driver in Austin who'd been placed in police custody after his employers found the remains of a local businessman in the trunk of his car. All the flesh had been gnawed from the man's bones. The cab driver died of starvation after one night in jail.

She scrolled through news report after news report, each more ghastly than the next, and below each were hundreds of comments from people speculating about a zombie apocalypse to wondering how they could get infected themselves.

"What have we done?" Sarai whispered. She looked up from the computer just as Dr. Trevor Adams walked in. She wanted to strangle him. Behind him, Dr. Vivaan stood, looking like he wanted to strangle her.

"Where's Ebersol?"

Trevor looked at Dr. Vivaan, who gave him a stern, unsympathetic glare. "He's handling a little problem. We had to chain down our two special patients. They kept breaking through their restraints. Their overactive adrenal glands have made them unusually strong. I'm afraid one of the nurses was severely bitten," Trevor said.

"She's dead. Her throat was ripped out by the model, Lelani Simms," Dr. Vivaan added, sweeping the room with his baleful gaze.

Sarai felt her stomach drop like she'd just fallen off a cliff. She swallowed hard, sucking down bile that scalded the back of her throat. "Where is she now?"

"On her way to the morgue, and I'm going back to India."

Sarai sighed and shook her head. "You may want to wait. I have something to say that may change your mind."

"What could you possibly say to me that would make me want to be a part of this insanity you've created here?"

"The virus has mutated. It's infectious."

The room fell silent.

"A-are you sure?" Trevor asked.

"Has anyone even bothered to look at the news today? It's everywhere," Sarai answered.

"Have they—have they traced it back to us?" Trevor asked.

"Not yet, but they will. Right now, they think it has something to do with AIDS."

"AIDS?"

"They think the HIV virus mutated, and that's what's causing the disease. I guess they traced the origin of the virus back to a guy who was HIV infected. I checked, and he wasn't a client of ours, but he'd recently received a new kidney from one of our clients who died in an auto accident."

Dr. Vivaan looked at Dr. Adams and shook his head. "And none of you ever thought of this possibility?" he asked.

Sarai was confused. "What possibility?"

"Tell her! Tell her what this virus of yours has done!" Dr. Vivaan was shaking with rage. Dr. Ebersol walked in and looked from the angry little Indian man to Trevor. They were all looking at Trevor, waiting for him to explain it all.

"Most likely, our retrovirus piggybacked onto the HIV retrovirus. That's how it's spreading."

"Spreading?" Ebersol asked.

"Yes, spreading. It's all over the news. And you knew this could happen?" Sarai asked, turning back to Trevor.

Trevor shrugged and held up his hands in surrender. "I didn't really think about it. We screened everyone we treated for HIV before we injected them. If that chef hadn't gotten himself killed and then donated his damn organs, the virus would still be contained."

"But it isn't contained anymore, now is it?" Ebersol snapped.

Screams came from beyond the door, down the hall. An alarm sounded. More screams. The doctors all looked at each other, hollow-eyed, the terror they felt etched plainly across each of their faces. Ebersol peeked out the door and looked down the hall. More screams echoed throughout the building, accompanied by guttural snarls and growling. It sounded like people were being slaughtered.

Ebersol looked at his watch. "What time were the other patients supposed to arrive?"

Sarai checked the time on her Smartphone. "They should have been here twenty minutes ago."

They all looked back toward the open door and slowly crept toward it, joining Ebersol and peering down the hallway. More screams filled the halls.

"Did you tell them to keep the patients restrained and sedated?"

"I-I don't know. I don't remember," Sarai replied.

"Well, it sounds like your patients have arrived," Dr. Vivaan said.

They retreated back into the room and closed the door. By silent agreement, Ebersol, Trevor Adams, and Vivaan began moving furniture. They slid Sarai's big oak desk in front of the door, and seconds later something struck it hard and began scratching at it, snarling like a wild beast. Everyone fell silent. The snarling sounds increased as others joined the party, slamming into the door, growling savagely, trying to claw right through the solid oak.

"Call the police," Ebersol whispered.

Sarai reached for her cell phone and punched in 060, the police emergency number in Cancun.

"Hola, policía de Cancun. ¿Cuál es su emergencia?"

"We're trapped in a room at the Aphrodite Aesthetic Reconstruction Clinic Resort. There are people trying to kill us! We need help!"

"Que?"

"Hay caníbales tratando de comer! Estamos en la Aphrodite Aesthetic Reconstruction Clinic. Prisa! Por favor! Ayuda!"

She hung up.

"What did you say?"

"I said there were cannibals trying to kill us."

"Are they coming?" Trevor asked. His eyes were wide with terror, listening to the things scratching at the other side of the door, things that had once been his patients.

"I think so."

There were more screams outside. Trevor and Ebersol walked over to the window. Dr. Vivaan hesitated and then joined them.

"Jesus Christ!"

Despite her reservations, Sarai joined her colleagues at the window and peered out. There were bodies strewn across the parking lot, body parts. White lab coats, nurses' shoes, the green jumpsuits worn by the gardening staff, the gray jumpsuits worn by the janitors, and a few civilian clothes, sundresses, khaki shorts, gym shoes, jeans, and T-shirts lay in bloody rags in front of the building. Some still had limbs inside them. One of the jumpsuits still contained a dismembered torso, the chest ripped open and hollowed out. Disembodied heads lay strewn about like a destructive child's discarded doll parts. Two bodies still looked relatively intact, and people were feeding on them.

Sarai recognized one of the assailants, the little girl, Star Mourning. Her teeth jutted out of her mouth, hanging down below her bottom lip like a saber-toothed cat. Her face was painted red with blood. She was on all fours, clawing at a man Sarai recognized as one of the orderlies, pulling out his insides and greedily feasting on them. Beside her, two other creatures Sarai didn't recognize tore the man's limbs off and casually stripped them of flesh, gnawing at the bones like a rack of barbecued ribs, smacking their lips and licking the blood and gore from their fingertips. Sarai turned away.

There was a loud crack, and everyone turned to look behind them at the barricaded door. It was starting to splinter. It wouldn't hold much longer. For the first time, Dr. Vivaan's face held an expression other than anger and disgust. He looked terrified.

He turned to Trevor, his mouth hanging open in shock. "You've killed us all, you dumb sonuvabitch. You've killed us all."

"We need to find something to arm ourselves with."

Everyone began looking around the room. There wasn't much. Sarai grabbed the letter opener. Ebersol hefted a wooden chair. It was too heavy to swing effectively. He smashed it against the floor several times until he had something small enough to work with, a chair leg with part of the armrest still attached. Trevor grabbed a piece of the chair, and so did Vivaan.

"Shit, I almost forgot!"

Sarai walked over to the desk, opened the drawer, and removed a large black semiautomatic pistol. "I've never used it. I forgot I had it in there."

"Glad you remembered it," Ebersol said. "Why do you have it anyway?"

Sarai shrugged. "You never know."

"Never know what? When a bunch of cannibals mutated with pygmy shrew DNA will come busting through your door?" Vivaan asked.

Sarai ignored him.

There was another cracking sound, and a thin brown arm thrust through a sizeable hole in the door and began scratching at it from the inside, gouging huge dents in the wood.

"That ain't gonna hold much longer," Trevor said.

"Really? Because I feel completely fucking safe!" Vivaan replied.

"You don't have to be a dick about it. We're all in this together."

Vivaan took several quick steps toward Trevor until he was practically chest to chest with the man. At five feet, five inches tall, he was a few inches shorter than Trevor and didn't have the young Dr. Adams's hormonally enhanced muscles, but Trevor took a step back and dropped his eyes, unable to meet the man's accusatory stare.

"We're all in this because you were stupid and irresponsible enough to think cross-species genetics was a good idea. Because you would use something this dangerous for the vanity of fat wealthy Americans!" He spat at Trevor's feet.

Ebersol stared at the thin brown arm trying to claw its way into the room. It was familiar.

"Lelani?" Ebersol gasped.

Sarai stabbed the arm with her letter opener. There was a howl of anguish, and then the arm quickly withdrew back through the hole. Another arm, this one bony and ghostly white, thick spidery blue veins pulsating beneath the pale skin, reached through the hole. Sarai stabbed that one as well. Finally, the sound of sirens filled the air. Everyone rushed to the windows again, except Sarai. She remained, aiming her gun at the door as it began to give way.

"One car? They sent one fucking car!" Vivaan yelled, banging on the window in frustration.

"Up here! We're up here!" Trevor yelled, banging on the window as well.

The door cracked again and someone crawled through the hole, someone with long oily hair and thick claws like a badger. Sarai shot it twice as it lunged for her. One bullet went in the thing's shin, crippling it but barely slowing it. The thing crawled forward on bony, spidery limbs, growling and hissing, baring long, crimson-tipped fangs. The second bullet went through the thing's neck. It fell to the floor, gargling its own blood but still reaching out for Sarai, still desperate for her flesh. Sarai shot it again, silencing it for good.

Someone—something—else crawled through the hole in the door.

"Help! Guys, help!"

"We're right here. Give me the gun," Ebersol said, lifting it from her hands as the emaciated thing with the tan skin and natty afro scrambled to its feet. Ebersol immediately recognized her. He'd loved her since the first day she'd walked into his office. It was his fault she was like this. He'd been blaming Trevor all this time, but the reality was he had brought her to him. He had recommended Trevor and had failed to protect her.

"They're attacking the cops! They're tearing them apart!" Trevor screamed. He was trembling, and urine stained the front of his pants.

Lelani shambled forward, and Ebersol lifted the gun. He aimed it at her forehead. "I love you, Lelani. I always have."

She paused and cocked her head. Ebersol's finger hovered over the trigger. Two more patients crawled through the crack in the door. The hole was no more than a foot wide, yet their emaciated bodies squeezed through easily. Ebersol heard Trevor scream, followed by ripping sounds and the sound of feeding. Vivaan cursed in Indian, followed by the sound of wood-splitting bone, a sound that repeated again and again.

"Shoot! Shoot!" Sarai cried out in a panic.

Ebersol gazed lovingly upon Lelani's once-beautiful countenance, now ravaged by starvation and soaked in the blood of his murdered coworkers. There was something sad in her expression, something desperate and agonized. He could only imagine what she was feeling as her body burned more calories than she could ever possibly consume, driven mad with a hunger she could never assuage. A tear spilled from the corner of his eye when she bared her red-tipped fangs, snarling.

"I love you, Lelani. I'm so sorry."

She roared and charged forward. He had the gun aimed right between her eyes.

But he never pulled the trigger.

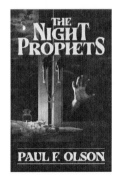

HORROR
DNA
MOVIES
COMIC BOOKS
MUSIC
BOOKS
VIDEO GAMES
IT'S IN
OUR
BLOOD
horrordna.com